" SMILEY "

Mary N. Maxwell

DEDICATION

This story was inspired by Terry T., a childhood classmate whose autism was not known at the time. This story is a tribute to him and all who have a similar form of challenge.

ACKNOWLEDGMENTS

My deep appreciation to Sandy Nachlinger, friend and fellow author, who edited my manuscript and offered advice that greatly improved my skills.

Many thanks to Marjorie Stanfield, who worked patiently with me to create my Smiley character for the Book Cover.

And immense gratitude for my family and friends who encouraged me to write my 'first' book!

♥

CHAPTER ONE

NICKI - 1978

Nicki was exhausted. Her last business trip had been intense and what would have been a two-day trip had turned into three full days. Her little condo had never looked better and she found the familiar very calming. Any other time, she would go straight to the bedroom, empty her neatly packed suitcase, and put everything in its proper place. Just this once, she thought, I will procrastinate. She set the suitcase at the closet entrance, kicked off her shoes, and collapsed across the bed.

Less than ten minutes later, the chaos around her outweighed her exhaustion. She arose and with the precision that is her reputation, began doing what she did not initially do. By rote, she lifted out the clothes that were still clean, hanging them carefully on the felt hangers, and pulling the steamer in the room, began to go over them until there was no hint of their travels. The soiled clothes were put in the basket and taken to the laundry closet, and though there was not enough for a full load, the washer was started. Returning to the bedroom, shoes were put in the boxes in the closet, but not before vacuuming and putting cedar sachets in each. The suitcase was also vacuumed and placed inside the closet, on the far left side, where it would stay until the next business trip. Looking around, everything was now in place and she felt like she could go into the kitchen and make herself a cup of tea. She really was exhausted and maybe the hot chamomile would relax and prepare her for a good night's sleep.

The night went quickly and she awoke totally refreshed, as sleeping only in one's bed can accomplish. After starting the coffee pot, she returned to the bathroom where she applied her make-up. Not much was required, for which she was thankful. Everyone who ever knew her told her she had natural beauty and, as she looked at her reflection, she couldn't help but wonder from whom she had acquired her features. She looked nothing like her parents and had always yearned to look more like her mother, who was a real beauty in her earlier years. Nicki's soft blue eyes were highlighted by the thick blonde pageboy hairstyle. Although that style was no longer in vogue, her hair just turned under naturally and required very little maintenance. She capitalized on that and really loved the bounce of her hair when she walked.

She returned to the kitchen and retrieved her coffee. Eager to get to the office, she poured out more than half of it, rinsed the cup, and made one more trip to the bathroom, to brush her teeth. She felt so fortunate to have healthy, straight and white teeth, and once she applied her red lipstick, she looked into the mirror and smiled, not just a slight smile, but the one she was famous for, the larger than life smile.

Grabbing her handbag, she did one last check of the kitchen. It was tidy, just as she would expect. She grabbed her keys and locked the door behind her. Let the day begin!

The bus arrived at the scheduled time and Nicki rewarded the driver with a smile. He winked back and she was pretty sure

3

it was not flirtatious but an acknowledgment that he had met her expectations by being punctual. She took her usual seat, near the center of the bus and next to the window. A feeling of comfort surrounded her as she watched the familiar buildings dash by. Forty minutes later, she stepped off the bus and walked one block to her destination of the day.

***

The Ad Agency, as it was simply known, had been her home away from home for the last eight years. On a lark, she'd responded to the lead from a bulletin in the hall of the university, just a week before being awarded her Master's Degree. Two weeks later, as she pored over the local newspaper, her mother had brought the envelope to her. The name on the return address did not at first seem familiar but once she said it aloud, she recalled mailing her resume.

Nervously, she slid her red nail under the sealed edge. She anxiously unfolded the contents and began reading. "Your resume is of some interest to us. We hope you will entertain the opportunity of a personal interview in our Houston office. Please contact our office with your expression of interest and we will make the necessary travel arrangements for you."

"Mom," she squealed, "I have a job!"

Once the reality set in, she reconsidered her statement. And then she thought how her life would change if this came to fruition. She had lived with her parents for the better part of twenty–three years, in a relatively small community in North Carolina, leaving only long enough to attend the university

4

which was two hours away. She was their only child and the center of their universe, so trips home were frequent and the many homecomings were always celebrated. Over the years, they had taken family vacations so she had seen other places, but she had never seen a cosmopolitan city like Houston. It never occurred to her that she might actually live there one day. Even as she penned a response, the notion seemed surreal.

Her written response was followed by a phone call to the office. As she identified herself, the receptionist became familiar toward her, as though she had been expecting her call.

"Oh, please call me Nicki," she said. "Nicole is so formal." The truth was, she had always gone by Nicole, so why she would suddenly take on a nickname was a little strange, but there it was. It popped out of her mouth before she knew it and now it was too late to retract it. She would henceforth be known as Nicki, and if things went right for her, she would be Nicki at The Ad Agency!

The trip for the interview was in two weeks and the "now known as Nicki" had a lot to do. Her parents were guardedly enthusiastic for her. Of course, they brought her up to be independent and they wanted her to be happy but they could not imagine their lives without their girl. And, who knew what the future would hold?

"Nicole," her mother said, "I think before you begin your new job, you should see our family doctor and get a thorough exam."

"Well, I don't actually have the job yet, but that's a good idea, Mother. I don't think I've had a real physical since before college. I will make an appointment tomorrow."

The following two weeks dragged by. She was able to get into the doctor's office where he had run her through the usual tests – urinalysis, blood work, etc. That out of the way, she returned to the planning of her trip.

What was thought of as a "lot to do" turned out to be very little. She would fly to Houston on the 15th, shuttle immediately to The Ad Agency's office, be interviewed, followed by a light lunch, and be taxied to the hotel for the night, returning home the following day.

Nicki - 1970

She packed light. She would wear a pencil skirt, a modest but crisp white blouse, and her favorite heels. It was important to her that she not just *look* the part but present an image of what they could expect should she be hired. Her bag consisted of night clothes, toothbrush, mascara, and slacks. She would wear the same blouse the following day. She felt a slight quiver in her stomach as her parents drove her to the airport.

Her mother, with a concerned smile, turned to Nicole in the back seat. "Nicole dear, you seem a bit tense. I know you are embarking on a journey, but see it as an adventure. You look lovely and confident. You will make quite an impression."

"Mother, you always know the right things to say. I will make every effort to be myself and hope that's enough." After hugs, she waved her parents off and waited for boarding. She thought she had detected a tear on her mother's cheek, but she may have been wrong, because both parents were upbeat and encouraging.

***

She walked to her seat in the middle of the plane, and as she made her way down the aisle, a couple of male business travelers took notice and gave her more than a glance. Blushing, she took her seat and prepared for take-off. Before departing, both gentlemen would turn their heads to see if they could elicit a hopeful glance. Unsure of how to act, she picked up a magazine and pretended to be immersed in the articles.

Exiting the plane, she made her way down the concourse and spotted the shuttle to the office. Being the only passenger, she wondered if she was the only one who had applied for the position. In less than thirty minutes, she was standing in front of the receptionist who acted as though she was her best friend. She was asked to take a seat, which gave her the opportunity to absorb her surroundings. Not wanting to appear anything but well-traveled, she kept an air of confidence as she glanced around at the lobby, which was massive and impressive, boasting floor-to-ceiling windows, leather seating, and tree-sized plants. Shortly, a tall, middle-aged and sophisticated looking man appeared from nowhere, introducing himself as Jack Dunlap. She followed him to a corner office on the same floor. The walls of his office were dotted with awards of excellence. For a moment, she considered a quick get-away, thinking that she might not be "excellent" material.

Declining his offer of coffee, she sat upright in her chair, crossing her long legs. She saw his quick glance toward them, but his even quicker look away. For the next hour, she was interrogated, answering questions that she never anticipated. Fortunately, she had researched the company and could ask some reasonably direct questions herself. Finally, both parties began to relax, but the interview had appeared to come to an end.

"Miss Boyer, if you have no more questions, I will walk you back to the reception area and Miss Farrell will summon transportation to your hotel."

That's it, she thought. No job offer; no expectation of a second interview? She found herself both relieved and perplexed as she traveled to the hotel, wondering if she had conducted herself professionally enough.

Her room was pleasant enough. The desk clerk had advised her that her room, dinner, and drinks were all paid in advance and if she required anything, she need only call. She kicked off her heels and a wave of tiredness washed over her. She opened the mini bar and took out a bottle of Perrier water. She would never have been so frivolous as to pay for designer water, but since her accoutrements were taken care of, she thought, why not?

Besides, she was quite sure that she was not being considered a candidate for the position, or there would have been some hint of a return trip.

Bored, she decided on an early dinner and slipped her shoes on and took the elevator to the hotel restaurant. Nothing on the menu appealed to her but she knew she had to eat, so she ordered eggs benedict and was pleasantly surprised at the preparation. Since her meal was comped, she left a very generous tip and waited to see the expression on her server's face. So far, it was her favorite part of the day.

When she returned to her room, her bed had been turned down. Then, in her peripheral vision she spotted something near the window.

A beautiful flower arrangement had been delivered. Thinking it was delivered to the wrong room, she grabbed the card. It was from Mr. Dunlap at The Ad Agency. *"Thank you for gracing us with your presence today. We hope your trip was enjoyable and we will be in touch."* Not sure how to interpret that, she just accepted the sentiment with which they were delivered.

She cleaned her face, took a warm shower, and took advantage of the thick, white terrycloth bathrobe provided by the hotel. Picking up the bottle of remaining water, she walked over to the wide window that overlooked the city. It was dusk and street lights lit up the paths of the people on the sidewalks. Some of the office buildings were still lit. She wondered if the lights in the Ad Agency were still shining brightly as employees worked to meet their deadlines. In the distance, she could see the highway, with traffic lined up for what appeared to be miles. Perhaps it was better if this did not work out, she thought. She already missed the slow and simple life of North Carolina.

***

Surprisingly, she slept well. She dressed quickly and went back to the restaurant where she had coffee and toast. Expecting to pay, she was told that it had been taken care of. Returning to her room to pack, she regretted that the flower arrangement had to be left behind and thought it careless of the agency to send something that they surely knew she could not take with her. Hopefully, housekeeping would get to enjoy it.

Soon, she was back in the airport. She was going home and she was ready. Mentally recapping her last eighteen hours, she thought, Who in the world would want that kind of life, the deadlines, the travel, the traffic? She was perfectly content in her little world and would find a job more suited to her lifestyle.

Aboard the plane, she closed her eyes as she summed up the day. She had been so optimistic and thought she had nailed the interview, but now felt empty about it.

***

Hiding the disappointment of her trip, she spotted her parents and pulled them in for a tight hug. With feigned excitement, she told them all about the impressive building of her would-be employer, the traffic, the lights, and her hotel. She was quite sure they had no idea that she was already resigned to a failed interview.

Hopeful

The next few weeks were agony. Though none was expected, she still waited for the phone call or a letter to arrive, even if it was a "Thank you for your interest, but we have found a more suitable applicant" response. She had resumed her job search but confined it to the more local vicinity.

Exactly three weeks later, the doorbell rang. She could hear her mother at the door. Her words of delight carried through the house. Curious, Nicole arose from the table, only to meet her mother face-to-face, as she carried an enormous flower arrangement toward her.

"Whoa, who died?" Nicole exclaimed.

"These are for you, Nicole, and aren't they beautiful?" She blinked, in awe of the largest arrangement she had ever seen.

Nicole rushed to her mother's side. "For me?"

There was a separate envelope which she took from her mother's outstretched hand. The return address was "The Ad Agency." Immediately, Nicole thought this was the most unusual manner in which to send a letter of regret. She read it three times while her mother hovered nearby. She almost collapsed into her chair. "Dear Miss Boyer, after due consideration, and the interview of several more candidates, we are pleased to offer you the position of Junior Ad Account Executive."

Her mother clapped her hands. "That's wonderful. I'm so pleased for you. Of course, there was never any question in my mind about the job!"

Nicole stared at the paper again and tried to absorb the words. "You won't believe this, Mom. They offered me a starting salary of forty-five-thousand dollars plus a commission for the first year. Forty-five-thousand. Can you imagine?"

"Oh, honey. All your years of schooling are paying off. What else does the letter say?"

"They're looking forward to my immediate response."

Her head was spinning. She had not only accepted that she had been rejected but was resigned, and perhaps a little comforted, by the thought that she would find something more suitable to her lifestyle and location. Now, she had to make a quick decision, which was not easy for someone as systematic as she was.

That evening, Nicole sat with her parents, as she deliberated on her options. Really, the choices were limited. Either take the career, or look for a job. There was a big difference in the two and her parents had invested in an education that would provide her the opportunity for a professional position. They encouraged her to do what she thought would be best for her and they never made her feel obligated to make a choice that was unsuitable.

Nicole weighed the pros and cons of taking the job in Houston and decided she would be foolish to reject such a generous offer. That was it. She cried to release the tears of tension and her parents cried because they knew they were facing a new chapter.

Her mom and dad then exchanged a nervous glance. Her dad cleared his throat and spoke. "That's a wise decision, Sweetie, but we sure will miss you. And, um, there's something we need to talk about. It's about—."

"Never mind," her mom interrupted. "We can discuss that later. Now let's celebrate your good news with ice cream." She glared at her husband and motioned the family to the kitchen.

***

In two weeks, Nicole sat in her father's station wagon, a road map in her lap. Her belongings filled the car's trunk, with more in her little Corolla which they towed. Her journey had begun. Saying good-bye to her mother was so difficult, and she knew that when it was time to do likewise with her father, it would be a repeat performance.

Her mother's small figure as seen from the side view mirror of the car soon disappeared, marking the reality of change.

Fifteen hours later, two very tired travelers pulled into a local motel on the outskirts of Houston. After six hours of much needed sleep, Nicole pulled out the information the agency had sent her. It was a bit overwhelming, maps showing where the office was located and notations of some of the apartments in a thirty-mile commute. She wanted to make a choice and get unloaded so she could get her father home. She could tell he was exhausted even though he gave her a reassuring smile whenever she inquired.

"Dad, let's just get some coffee and a quick breakfast and check out these apartment recommendations. I want to get you on the road."

"Don't fret over me, Nicole. This will likely be my only opportunity to see Texas. Your dad is not as old as you think. I will be fine," he said with a wink.

The first apartment was not at all what she was expecting and with some disappointment, they drove to the next one. As it turned out, this was a condominium that was a Rent to Own, but the unit was perfect. It was upstairs and in the back of the complex, and appeared to be clean and quiet. Partly because she wanted her father to get home and partly because it seemed all right, she signed the paperwork and the unloading began. The bedroom furniture was assembled and the rest was deposited in the large living area, to be put away later. Her main objective was for her dear father to get on the road, especially before the rush hour traffic began.

"Dad, let me make you something for the trip."

"And what would that be, dear daughter? You have no food except for the snacks we picked up along the way. And quit fussing over me. I will stop at a diner when I need to eat. Now, come give your dad a good-bye hug and a kiss on the cheek." With tears in her eyes, she stood at the door, watching him drive away.

She dug into the boxes to find the sheets for the bed and the coffee maker, and got those two chores done. She had put her night clothes into her overnight bag so quickly showered and surveyed the work ahead of her but decided that a good night's sleep would have to come first.

The Boyers

In North Carolina, her parents had gotten a call from the doctor's office. They had received all of Nicole's test results from her physical but did not have her new address. Mrs. Boyer, very familiar with the nurse, could not resist telling her the good news.

"Miss Strickland, did our Nicole tell you about her new adventure? She has secured a new career and will be living in Houston. We are so proud of her."

"Oh, yes, Mrs. Boyer," she said in a rushed tone, "Nicole did share her good news. That's why I need her new address, so that we can mail her results!"

"Forgive me, of course. She will receive mail at 115 Station Road, Houston, Texas 77005."

The conversation ended abruptly as Mrs. Boyer realized she was intruding on the nurse's busy schedule.

CHAPTER TWO

SMILEY - 1940

There he goes again. It's repetition that you can count on. Day after day, Pete, who we call "Smiley," comes into town. It is always the same. He walks into each store, wearing that big smile that earned his nickname and asks, "Any work for me today?" The expected question is met with the expected answer, "Not today, Smiley, maybe tomorrow." As sure as the sun rises on the following day, the pattern is repeated. Oh, it's not because he remembers that there *might* be work. It's just the routine that gives him comfort. One of these days, a store owner is going to ask him if he wants to help unload supplies or sweep the floor and honestly, I don't think he will even process that. That's Smiley.

Peter Aaron Jameson was born in 1925, to James Aaron and Henrietta Sue Jameson. They were a sweet but older couple, reconciled to the fact that they would never have children, so when little Pete was born, it was not just a surprise to the community but to the couple. They doted on their little boy. In fact, they had such great love for their son, they didn't even notice that he demonstrated early signs of being different from other kids his age.

Smiley was the happiest of children. His smile was the testimony of that. When he was old enough to walk, he began to develop routines. Oh, not routines like you and I have, but routines with very distinctive patterns. After breakfast each morning, he would go to the garden.

Henrietta had an enviable garden. In fact, she had two gardens, one on either side of the house. One was filled with vegetables of every variety and the other with an array of flowers that any florist would covet. Smiley loved the vegetable garden. He would start in the same spot each morning, and walk from the beginning of a row to the very end. Then, rather than going from there to the next row, he would run all the way to where he had begun, and repeat the process on the next row. There were twelve rows, and he would take the same path three times each morning. Never did anyone see him walk through the other garden.

I remember asking him one day, "Smiley, don't you want to walk through that beautiful flower garden?" The response was nonverbal and it was the only time I've seen Smiley frown. He then walked right over to the vegetable garden to repeat the process that was so comfortable for him.

I was drawn to Smiley. Everyone was. But I lived alone, and just a stone's throw from the Jameson's so I had not only the time but the desire to be around them. They had become my second family. Besides, I thought it might help if Smiley had someone to hang around with since James and Henrietta were always consumed with the upkeep of the fields, the animals, and the home chores. I became Smiley's surrogate big brother.

When Smiley was six, he started school. I would watch from my window as he carried his lunch bag with him as Henrietta escorted him to the school bus. Most of the time he was barefoot, as was the custom of children in the country, at least until winter. He, of course, was smiling as his mama kissed him on the cheek and sent him on his way. I missed our mornings together, and his routine in the vegetable garden, but I was happy to see that he could actually forego his comfort zone and begin school.

In fact, I began to think that I had perhaps been observing little Smiley with too critical an eye. I had just about reconciled in my mind that his daily rituals were a sign of something more….or less…as I thought the case might be. Here he was, going to school, and quite comfortably so. Then there was high school.

My suspicions began to ring true. As soon as Smiley began high school, it was obvious that he was "different." He just could not connect to any of the required classes. In fact, the only class in which he was proficient was math, and specifically the multiplication tables. And did he ever excel at those. Everyone was amazed at how he could multiply, and all in his head. Everywhere he went, he was multiplying. He would see pricing signs in stores and multiply all the numbers. We were both amazed and confounded. How could someone be so accomplished in this skill, and have so little aptitude for the other classes?

My interest in Smiley intensified. I was no longer playing the role of big brother, but I had now taken on the role of teacher and mentor. I could tell that Smiley had a unique mind, but I could also see that he was really lacking in the common sense that propelled a child to adult. While this was evident to me, James and Henrietta would have none of it. They were nothing but proud of their boy. They would sit on their rockers on the porch for hours in the evening, just listening to their Smiley recite the multiplication tables.

***

Smiley was still getting on the bus each day and going through the routine of school, but it was obvious that he could not graduate. Late one morning, Smiley was removed from his class and the Vice Principal told him he was going to drive him home. Smiley, wearing his big smile, excitedly climbed into the car and experienced his first automobile ride, all without realizing what awaited him at home. The driver, realizing I had a deeper understanding of Smiley's personality than his parents did, pulled me aside to tell me it was evident that Smiley could not possibly graduate and was becoming a distraction to this classmates. He had made the decision to take him out of school for good. I acknowledged my agreement.

Several days later, after hearing a blood-curdling cry in the direction of the Jameson's, I made a beeline to their house. In the front yard, right in front of the vegetable garden, Henrietta stood over James, who was lying face down.

Though I rushed to his side, it was too late to do anything. James had taken his last earthly breath. As I consoled Henrietta, Smiley ran up to us. He took one look at James and smiled, then walked slowly into the house.

At the funeral and afterwards, at the house, full of neighbors bearing food, Smiley did what Smiley did best. He smiled. For several weeks, as I stayed close by to help Henrietta, I saw no sign that Smiley had understood the loss of his father.

Smiley, out of habit, returned to school, but was told he could not continue. He walked home and waved to his mama but Henrietta never said a word. She neither encouraged nor discouraged school. Quite honestly, she had just lost interest in everything.

One day, out of the blue, Henrietta called me into the house.

"It's time for Smiley to learn how to hunt." She handed me the old gun that I had seen James hold a hundred times. "Will you teach him?"

I had serious reservations, but I knew not to question Henrietta. I reluctantly took the gun and nodded my head in the direction of the woods. A wide-eyed Smiley followed me.

Early the next morning, I walked over and, as I had done many times before, waited for Smiley to complete his ritual walk among the vegetable garden, which had become sorely neglected. We then proceeded to the woods. I had taken some old cans for target practice and lined them up on a row of old stumps.

"First," I told Smiley, "you must learn how to respect a gun. There are ways to hold it and ways to shoot it. You have to pay attention to each step I show you." I had a suspicion that I would have to repeat this process several times, but in true Smiley fashion, he surprised me. He took quickly to the lessons, and when we were finally ready to shoot the targets, he took careful aim and did not miss one. I guess you know what came next. Yes, that monumental smile. He wore it proudly, as well he should. I was more than pleasantly surprised by his skill and the way he had handled the gun.

For the next few weeks, we hunted regularly and he did not disappoint his mama when he brought home squirrel and rabbit for dinner.

"Mama, mama," he declared. "I am a good shooter. See what I did." He would proudly display his kill for the day.

"That's a good boy. Your mama is proud of you." Henrietta barely gave him a glance. She was always busying herself with chores.

Smiley and Henrietta had more or less settled into a life without James. The little farm was suffering and I did all I could do to help. Henrietta did not have time to grieve. She was busy tending to not only her daily chores but the ones that her beloved James had managed as well. Smiley was there, but he was now fixed on hunting. I noticed that he had even skipped his garden routine a couple of times.

In 1944, we received word that the country was at war. There was an all-out effort to recruit all young men to fight. I admit that I was a little relieved that I was well beyond the age of service, so life, as Henrietta, Smiley and I knew it, continued.

Then, the unthinkable happened. That day, that one day that I had taken Smiley to town and he was asking the merchants for work, he walked into the recruiting station. He told me later that he had seen a sign with a young man his age in uniform and said he wanted to be just like the boy in the window sign. He had asked the recruiter if he had any work for him and before he knew it, he had joined the Army. Smiley had finally gotten someone in town to "give him work."

We were halfway home when he told me and I realized I must turn straight around and explain to the recruiter that Smiley was not qualified. I began to try to explain to Smiley why he could not serve, but he had made up his mind, and as with anything that young man wanted to do, there was no changing it.

When we got to the farm, I explained to Henrietta what had happened.

"Henrietta, I think you should know that Smiley went to the Army Recruiting Station today and signed up."

"Oh, that's a good thing he did," she said proudly. I realized that she had no real notion that Smiley might be a little addled.

"Henrietta, I think I should pay a visit to the recruiter and explain why Smiley is not military material.

Adamantly, Henrietta said, "You will not. He will do exactly what he should do. My boy is going into the Army."

***

The next few weeks, I tried to prepare Smiley for what awaited him. I don't think he ever really got the concept and when Henrietta and I waved to him as he took off on the train, I don't think I've ever seen him happier. It was probably the fact that he was on the train, but of all the smiles I'd seen him wear, this had to be one of the biggest.

Each week thereafter, I fully expected to hear from Henrietta that he had been released and was on his way home, but it didn't happen. I was concerned. I couldn't imagine that Smiley had been able to conform to military life, but it then occurred to me that the military demanded routine and I knew how comforting that might be to him.

Months passed. I spent most of my time at Henrietta's, partly because she needed my help and mostly, because I wanted to be there if any word of Smiley arrived. But day after day, there was no mail and no Smiley. Our days were filled with routines of our own.

A year and four months had passed. We had quit hoping for Victory Mail from Smiley or his commanding officer, and had settled into the domestic routine of a couple, though we were anything but that. I had given up any possibility of getting married and having my own family. Henrietta needed me and Smiley would need me when he returned. And I confess, I needed *them*.

CHAPTER THREE

FRANCE - 1944

Spring in France should be enjoyed. We were engaged in an area more suitable to romance than to battle. The trees were giving in to a slight breeze and the smell of wildflowers surrounded us. It would have been reminiscent of a day in the country, but bullets were flying in all directions.

We were told to return fire but protect ourselves. Therein was the challenge. As Platoon Sergeant, I wanted to secure our position but the enemy outnumbered us threefold. The field operator was shouting into the radio but with the noise of the surrounding ammunitions firing, he could not hear the command. With a slight shake of the head, I acknowledged my understanding.

Suddenly, I saw a lanky figure ahead. His presence seemed to signal that he had found a path through the fortress of fire. He turned to indicate movement ahead. By golly, that was Smiley. He was actually giving his comrades that broad grin of his. I resisted calling his name or attempting to secure him. I knew by now that Smiley had his own agenda.

When he had first come into my command, his boot camp drill instructor accompanied him. He had explained to me that Smiley had enlisted and while he had significant reservations about his ability to serve, Smiley had really set the bar for his marksmanship. Furthermore, he was able to follow orders, stay in formation, and be an example for his comrades, and the only problem was the incessant counting as he completed each set of four steps. Initially, all his camp mates had frowned on his admission to the unit, but as time progressed, ol' Smiley turned all of us around. He never struggled with the obstacle course or the gun range and when he had completed the routine, rewarded all of us with that bigger-than-life smile of his.

When basic training was completed, the orders for deployment came quickly. In all the days of my training, I had never had a team so cohesive, and thanks to Smiley, seemingly happy. I had received notice that I would be leading a platoon of two-thirds of the group, the other third being assigned elsewhere. The war had escalated and it was "all boots on the ground." The German insurgence into France was ramping up and the Allies were being called in for help. I called the men together and informed them that we would be flown to Carbonne in the next few days, and would go from there into our post in Toulouse, in the south of France.

The next day, the recruits received their military rankings. When the name, Peter Jameson was called as Private, no one had stepped forward. My superior had given me a look, suggesting that one of the recruits was AWOL for the ceremony. That was when I realized that our Smiley had unwittingly not responded to his formal name.

I whispered to the Instructor, "Sir, please address him as Private Smiley and I will explain later."

With some hesitation and abandonment of formality, the

Drill Sergeant did as suggested, and when Smiley heard his name, he was nudged by one of his buddies to step forward. He smiled broadly and, forgoing standard military protocol, his entire platoon smiled along with him. I will never forget that occasion and while I was so proud that this rather eccentric young man had met all the physical requirements of training, I could not help but wonder if he could possibly survive a combat situation.

***

In exactly three days, we found ourselves on a military transport plane. I looked at all my men, dressed in their military fatigues. Some were engaged in casual chatter but most were pensive and somber, sensing what awaited in a land very foreign to them. The injury and death count was reported daily on the news, and none wanted to be one of those numbers, a casualty of war. I did not tell them the odds were against them. I glanced down the aisles again. There sat Smiley, the only one who appeared to be happy. Would he be the first to go down? He had no idea of the magnitude of what was ahead of him.

At 0200 hours, we were over the jump site. The tail of the plane opened slowly and I signaled the men to prepare. Their eyes locked with mine as if pleading me to change course. Smiley had been assigned to Pfc George Henderson. They would jump tandem. This was the one exception to the training Smiley had received. I first thought that not having him complete the jump training would result in his exclusion of service, but I was told, "Make it work. We need men." So this was the plan and George, who was both protective and fond of Smiley, volunteered immediately.

I looked up. The red light had changed to green and I began sending off each of my men, not knowing if I would ever see them again. I said a "God Bless You" to each as they disappeared in the dark abyss of the night.

As usual, just before George and Smiley took flight, I got that big toothy grin from Smiley. If he had any fear, it wasn't evident. I wondered if he could tell that I had fear for him.

I was the last one to jump and because of the darkness, I could spot no other parachutes. When I landed, I realized I was in close proximity to one of the men.

A sense of relief was followed by more anxiety. How could we unite in this darkness? But slowly, one-by-one, we began discovering each other. After what seemed like forever, we knew we were missing two, George and Smiley.

We huddled together in a depression in the ground until morning. Sleep was scant and only exacerbated the fear we felt upon waking. We quietly ate one of our meager breakfast rations and wished for some hot coffee, but we could not take a chance of the aroma permeating the air. After a quick briefing, we decided to walk two klicks in different directions, hoping to find our lost comrades. After approximately twenty minutes, I heard the soft sound of the "cricket" and proceeded to follow it. Because we were all about the same distance, we met at the same area at the same time. One of the guys pointed up to a large tree. I stifled a laugh. Swaying quite comfortably and quietly were George and Smiley, one of them wearing his trademark expression. A couple of the guys climbed up the tree and cut them loose while the rest of us positioned ourselves to break their fall. For the moment, the entire unit was together.

The acrid scent of gunpowder filled the morning air. We knew we were in an action zone but it was unsure how much time had passed since nearby battle had taken place. I had our radio guy signal the battalion I thought might be in the area. A response came back immediately. The team had taken casualties and they needed support. We radioed back that we were less than a half day away and would provide assistance. Things were getting real.

I called the guys together and gave them a pep talk. "This is what we trained for, men. It is OK to be afraid. That will make you more alert." I knew it wasn't the talk of a combat veteran, but for these farm boys, it seemed appropriate conversation.

Together, but some distance between every two men, we proceeded to the front line. There was an uncomfortable stillness in the air. Fear had spoken quietly and deeply.

We'd hiked about an hour along a rutted dirt road when we heard gunfire—loud and constant. We pushed on, and now with more motivation. Within no time, we joined the battle. The enemy was hidden, but their bullets came from all directions. I could not imagine coming out of this dogfight without losses and, in between the rounds, I said a prayer. "Dear God, please protect these men as they honorably serve their country."

Loading, shooting, reloading—I had no time to observe.
More than once, I looked into the eyes of my aggressor and
saw hate. I guess that was good because I was doing a job I
did not like and if I had seen fear, I may have had
compassion. I could have been the one wounded or worse,
killed.

After several hours, gunfire became more sporadic and then
stopped. The air looked like fog but smelled of sulfurous
smoke and singed bodies. I walked through the battleground
to survey the condition of my troops. A medic was working
on the arm wound of one of my men, but all the others were
without injury and, for the most part, stood around sharing
cigarettes and comparing war stories. Smiley was sitting on a
tree stump. Not seeing a smile on his face was a rarity. He
was busy counting the ammo in his belt. The corners of my
mouth turned up. I would not have picked this young man as
a soldier but he had surprised me on more than one occasion.
Whether from his training or from his affliction, he was
immersed in the exercise. He would be prepared for the next
surge of action even if his comrades weren't.

I visited with the other platoon leader who had lost two more
men and had several injured. He was surprised and I
thought, a little surly that our group had come out with only
one minor injury. I received his excuses with respect, telling
him that it was sometimes just the luck of the draw. In my
heart, I knew I had a team of exemplary soldiers. They
trained to the degree of perfection and, on the battlefield,
they had shown grit and determination.

We located a secluded area and all the guys enjoyed an MRE

of meat loaf. How I wished I could give them a meal befitting the work they had just done, but there were no complaints. They knew what they had signed up for. We all did.

We found a clearing and the men bedded down for the night while five sentries stayed on watch for three-hour shifts. Truth be known, not much sleep took place. In the darkness, the enemy could return and retaliate in a heartbeat. Sleep eluded me, too. I was up before the sun and wondered what the day would bring.

***

Orders were received by 0800, to travel to the small town of Capens. With no vehicles or tanks, foot soldiers were pulled together. We said our farewells to the platoon who had not yet received their orders. We formed our traditional groups and trod ahead. I walked behind, proud of my men.

We walked all day, stopping only once to eat and take care of personal business. The countryside was extraordinarily beautiful, replete with blossoming trees and colorful vines. We were astonished at some of the chateaus of the once wealthy and the *maisons de maitre* of the bourgeois villages. We had to keep our distance, for fear the enemy may have taken cover there, but we could not resist the urge to feast on the beauty of the flower gardens and charm of the homes. I was struck by the paradox of beauty and battle.

Toward dusk, and with miles to go, we saw what we would have called a lean-to, in the States. It was isolated and appeared to be vacant. I sent two of my men to check it out while the rest of us reconnoitered the areas around it. I got the all clear and decided that we had been given a gift, a respite from the elements of nature. We all piled in and released the weight of gear from our shoulders. One of the men saw a small closet or pantry and cautiously opened the door. He let out a whoop, spun around, and held up two bottles of wine. We all hovered around him and checking out the closet, found several more bottles. They had obviously been there for quite some time, but they were sealed tightly. All the men looked my direction, eyes begging for permission to open the bottles. My first reaction was to say no because if we came under attack, we needed to be at our best, but seeing the imploring looks of my men, with a nod, relented. I warned my troops that overindulgence would not be tolerated and that each soldier would be required to perform his share of sentry duty with military precision and alertness. The men readily agreed.

Before I knew it, the wine was flowing and the men were singing. I did not want to jeopardize my authority, but decided this was a moment when we could all be on equal ground. I became one of my men. When it was time to shift watch duty, the men were receptive and to the point that it was not even obvious that they had been drinking. The responsibility they exhibited confirmed that I had made the right decision. Fatigue had now set in and everyone found a place on the floor or huddled against the wall for a few hours of shut eye. I, too, found a small but relatively comfortable corner. The noise of the previous day gave way to an almost uncomfortably peaceful night.

The following morning began a little later. The men had slept soundly and weren't ready for an early morning reveille. I let them enjoy their slumber because I had no idea what was up the road.

***

We said good-bye to our little retreat, strapped on our packs and checked our weapons. We fell into our usual walking positions.

We had not gone far before we saw a young chap on a bicycle heading our direction. All the men but me took quick cover among the trees and bushes lining the road. I was driven by curiosity and kept my position. The boy had no reserve at all. He rode right up to me, gave me a weak salute and began speaking in French. I tried to tell him that I spoke no French, but he kept speaking and was gesturing wildly, his voice rising. I signaled my men that all was clear and we all gathered round the boy. One of the men suggested that the boy was trying to warn us, but of what? He acted as though he was counting. This piqued Smiley's interest and he pushed the men aside to get closer to the boy. In no time, it was like they had their own language, conversing not in French, but in a manner of understanding that required no particular language. The conversation wound down and the boy took his place on the bicycle, said "*soldier good*," and pedaled off.

Smiley began to walk away when I summoned him back. "Smiley, what did that young boy say to you?" I asked.

He said, "Men up ahead with guns," and he took his place among the guys. He had hardly a reaction, something I still

had not fully understood about him. Trusting he had
somehow translated what the boy had communicated, I
directed the men to be alert and ready for combat ahead.

In less than two hours, we were involved in a skirmish. I
won't call it a battle because it was almost an accident. We
surprised a group of German soldiers engaged in a visit of
sorts and when they got wind of our impending presence,
they took up their arms and began firing, although randomly.
They were quick to recognize that we outnumbered them and
they dispersed into the woods. No one on either side was
even grazed by a bullet.

***

We were again on the march. That evening, we arrived at our
destination. We stopped on the outskirts of the small French
village of Toulouse, which was situated in the shape of a
horseshoe. The town seemed rather innocuous and there was
no sign of life except for a couple of stray cats meandering
down the narrow main thoroughfare. We did not approach
it, but kept our position. After a good thirty minutes, I
ordered a few men to move in closer, but not to enter the
buildings.

They flanked the structures, but with quiet surveillance. They
all returned with the news of no activity. Still, I was guarded.
This could very well be an ambush. The enemy could be
waiting inside and thinking we thought all was clear, shoot
every one of us if we entered any of the cottages and
buildings. I decided that we needed to do something to draw
them out if they were indeed there. I ordered some of the

men to fall back half a klick and engage in a mock skirmish. If there were any Germans in hiding and they thought there was an engagement of the enemy, they might follow suit. The plan worked. After only a few minutes of gunfire, Germans began firing out the windows and doors of their cover. We moved in, finding shelter along the way.

My eyes spotted Smiley, who was displaying his marksmanship. Three Germans fell in quick succession from Smiley's gunfire. A rather lengthy battle ensued. For three or four hours, my ears rang from the sound of gunfire and blasts from exploding grenades. Shrapnel flew from shattered walls and windows and littered the once-pristine streets of Toulouse with rubble. Little by little, our unit prevailed. At last the few Germans who were left raised their arms in surrender, and we disarmed them. As we had no way to secure the prisoners, we reluctantly released them.

After a thorough search of the village, we were confident that it was empty, so we took time to look for areas that offered enough protection that we could get another good night's sleep. Nerves were on edge and adrenalin was still flowing, so little rest was had. We had once again come out of battle unscathed, and were feeling the joy of victory and another day of life.

***

The following day, new orders arrived. Germans were staying one step ahead of us and had invaded the little village of Sarlat, which was not too far from Paris. Once again, we were marching toward war.

We arrived to an involved conflict. No time was available for coordination. We fell into defense mode. The intense fire kept us pinned down until one of our cruiser tanks rumbled onto the scene. Within minutes, its 75 mm gun took charge. When the engagement was over, the village was one of ruin, bodies strewn across the cobblestone pavement. Twelve German soldiers were killed and four American souls lay dead. Three of my men were wounded, one significantly. We were able to extract the one who required more than field treatment and a medic administered aid to the other two. Men gathered to bow their heads as words were spoken over the four men before they were taken to a base camp. Our platoon regrouped and we somberly took to our positions in one of the remaining ruins of the village. We were all exhausted. We had fought for some consecutive days and we needed a break, but this was war. I again reminded myself that this is what we signed up for.

Evening found men from four different platoons trying to get rest. During the night, battle cries echoed off the stone walls-soldiers reliving the day's fight in troubled dreams. Morning could not come fast enough.

***

Word of the extended conflict had gotten back to the Base Commander and I had been summoned to the radio to take his call. He was both courteous and succinct in his assessment of our performance in the protracted battle. He congratulated me on the effort of our platoon and the support we had provided. He also expressed his surprise in the few injuries our team had incurred, insisting it was a mark of leadership. I protested, giving my men the credit and he finally acquiesced that they were skilled in their mission. I meekly asked about some personal time off and after a considerable silence on the other end, he finally agreed. He suggested that since we were close to Paris, and there were no enemy personnel in the vicinity at present, that we should march on to the city, and have a twenty-four hour R&R.

Happy to have good news for a change, I pulled the troops together to communicate the reward to them. The once somber and drawn faces transitioned quickly to smiles, laughs, and big bear hugs all around. For the most part, these men were boys from farming communities and never in their wildest dreams did they ever think they would be going to Paris.

The next morning, we located a creek where we could bath and shave. The water was cool and the morning pleasant. We ate our breakfast rations like it was biscuits and gravy with bacon. For the first time in a long while, laughter punctuated my men's conversations as we began our walk to Paris.

The beauty of the City of Lights took our breaths. Some of the guys had never heard of landmarks such as the Eiffel Tower or the Arc de Triomphe yet here we were, like tourists on a sightseeing trip. The historic buildings were massive and ornate. The men, in awe of the magnificence, also took notice of the abundance of beautiful young women. They were literally everywhere and they were not timid. They flashed smiles of red lipstick and sultry looks at the men as they attempted to communicate in their native language.

We all took ourselves to a local bar and began consuming a "loosening agent." Smiley sat off by himself until George walked over and grabbed him at the elbow, admonishing him for his solitude. He reminded him that they were in Paree and that he needed to relax and indulge in the festivities. I doubt that Smiley had any idea what was meant by all that, but soon, he had a large mug of beer in front of him and, at the urging of his fellow soldiers, began to drink up. As one drink was consumed, it was replaced by another. None of us was feeling much pain.

One of the wilder boys in the group decided it was time to take it to the next level. "Men," he yelled out, "let's go see how friendly them ladies really are." Whoops and whistles filled the room as the men started piling out the door. Smiley, unknowingly, and fairly tipsy, followed along. On the street, the men quickly found dames, as they called them. The women were all too happy to accommodate the needs of men in uniform, being lonely themselves as their men had been called to war.

The pairs began disappearing around corners and up the stairs of the flats. I glanced behind my shoulder to see a beautiful young creature with her arm through Smiley's, as she led him away.

My intuition told me to rescue him, but I was suddenly being embraced by another beauty, and quite frankly, I decided I should just let go and enjoy myself as well. For all I knew, we could all be called to our Maker in a battle tomorrow.

***

The next day found thirty or so men in a blissful state of mind, although their heads pounded from the amount of alcohol consumed the day and night before. They were all in agreement that this experience had been the time of their lives. If tomorrow never came, they were happy NOW.

The young lady who had secured Smiley for the night headed my direction. She had Smiley by the hand and more or less, handed him to me. At the same time, she placed a note in my other hand. Without opening it, I put it in my pocket.

I sauntered over to Smiley and said, "How was your evening, boy?"

He looked down at his hands and showed no emotion. "I need to check my ammo, sir."

"I'm sure it's fine."

With a sad look on his face, he shook his head, reached for his weapon, and began his comfortable routine. "It's my job, sir."

I decided to back off. I just hoped he had experienced an encounter with someone who had been gentle with his body and his spirit.

After an exhilarating twenty-four hours, we began our walk back to our assignment, but we did so with a spring in our steps.

CHAPTER FOUR

NICKI - 1970

Nicki had received correspondence from the doctor's office in North Carolina and was perplexed to read that a second blood test needed to be done. Her blood type had not matched either parent and they were sure there had been an error in processing. She was busy getting accustomed to life in the city, understanding the culture of the company, and making a few friends. She decided this could wait.

She had received her first assignment, to fly to Dallas and meet with a potential client. Mr. Dunlap had called her into his office and made a quirky little comment about the bird leaving the nest. She wasn't sure if he was making fun of her or trying to make her comfortable with the assignment he was describing. She decided to assume the latter.

Nicki knew that all the experienced team of reps were committed to other assignments. She was still surprised when Mr. Dunlap told her she would be assigned to the client.

"Sir?"

"We've scheduled you for a visit with a potential client in Dallas." He went on to describe the assignment. "Capturing the business of this customer would be significant to the Agency. We've pursued their business over the years, but they seemed to be content with their existing marketing firm." He smiled. "It was both a surprise and a compliment when we received a call, saying they were considering a change and wanted us to give them a proposal."

Not wanting to appear rattled, Nicki merely nodded. "Thank you for your confidence in me, sir."

Later, Nicki overheard Mr. Dunlap tell another agent, "Our little Nicki has to start somewhere." Based on the rest of his comments, he obviously hadn't realized that his experienced reps were all committed to other assignments, and he wished Nicki's first assignment hadn't been with such an important potential client.

Nicki was told that she needed to not only research the client but to also gather information on their current agency. That advice was one of the fundamental things in which she had been educated but she certainly did not undermine her superior by mentioning that. She simply nodded her head in agreement. To her surprise, Mr. Dunlap asked her if she would like to do some role-playing after she had done her research but before she met with the client. Somewhat insulted yet aware of the complexity of her assignment, she assured him that she felt very comfortable making a presentation to the potential client.

The next few days Nicki was immersed in study. The client's existing firm was a fixture in the Dallas market and their reputation was impeccable. With so much success, why would they change ad agencies? As she began to dig into their current arrangement, she could see no flags that would dictate changing agencies.

The day of Nicki's flight arrived sooner than expected. Her level of angst was at an all-time high. She had spent days of research and study and had found no reason for the client to entertain the notion of changing their agency. Still, she worried that she had missed something notable. Since she was a small girl, she had always been thorough in everything she did but felt a little unprepared for what was ahead.

Boarding the plane, Nicki counted the rows as she walked down the aisle. Counting rows was a habit she had since elementary school and she was almost unaware of the routine. She took a seat in the middle, since seats were unassigned. She was in a comfort zone, knowing that she was in the approximate center of the plane. She closed her eyes and tried to relax as the plane filled.

Into the short flight, she opened her eyes when a well-groomed man tapped her on the arm to ask permission to take the seat next to her. Nodding her head with approval, he politely stepped over her feet and put his briefcase on the floor in front of him. He began to explain that he had been seated next to a woman with an unhappy baby and he appreciated that she allowed him to escape. An awkward laugh was exchanged.

As they approached Dallas, she felt his gaze on her. She shifted in her seat to avoid his glance. She was much too absorbed in her upcoming performance than to participate in senseless engagement with someone she would never see again. In a matter of minutes, the flight attendant announced that the flight was descending and would be in Dallas in ten minutes.

Her stomach knotted as she felt the enormity of what was before her.

She was not staying over in Dallas, so was quickly able to hail a cab at the curb and provide the address of the destination. She had never seen the city and wanted to take in the ambiance, but she was so preoccupied with the upcoming presentation it was difficult to focus on the surroundings. There seemed to be a slower-paced nature to the city than she had experienced in Houston, but at such a quick observation, she may have been wrong. She just knew that life in Houston was not at all what she had expected. There seemed to be a constant need to get somewhere and the traffic confirmed it.

***

Nicki's arrival at the client's office was punctual, as planned. Actually, she was at the reception desk twenty minutes early. That was her idea of punctuality. Never in her life had she arrived anywhere at exactly the time expected. She considered it a professional courtesy to be early.

Taking her seat in the waiting room, she surveyed the name of the company, as it appeared on the wall and the logo below it. It was impressive. If their current agency had a role in that, they knocked it out of the park. Once again, she wondered why she was here.

At ten minutes after the scheduled appointment, a well-dressed older woman stepped in front of her and announced that Mr. Steinham would see her. There was no smile or familiar tone but just a matter-of-fact statement. Nicki wondered if she knew why she was there and if she felt some allegiance to their current agency and therefore resented her presence. She followed the woman into the bank of elevators and she pressed a button that said Executive Elevator. Her stomach was suddenly full of butterflies so she stood a little straighter, not wanting to give in to the nerves.

Stepping off the elevator, the nerves returned. She noticed offices in each corner of the floor. They approached a set of double doors and an impressive gold nameplate that read, Leonard Steinham, President and CEO. The doors opened to reveal what looked like a penthouse apartment with a massive peninsula desk as the focal point. Behind it was a credenza filled with company memorabilia and family photos.

Mr. Steinham introduced himself and said, "Miss Boyer, please be seated."

Nicki took a seat in an uncomfortable and oversized tufted leather chair. It suggested to her that more men than women were guests in this office. The click of the door closing behind her signaled the departure of the assistant who had led her into the office.

Perhaps sensing her discomfort, he offered pleasantries. "How was your flight? Is this your first visit to Dallas?"

She answered with honesty and brevity, and included compliments about his building and his opulent office. Once they'd dispensed with the preliminary conversation, Nicki decided to take the liberty to question him. "Mr. Steinham, we are most pleased that you have given us the opportunity to secure your advertising business. To what do we owe this consideration?"

He clasped his hands on his desk and leaned forward. "Well, young lady, we have settled into a complacent relationship with our existing ad company. We thought it might be time to see if someone could interject some new blood into the company." He chuckled.

The butterflies in her stomach began to settle. Now she understood. "And to what degree might our firm offer that, Mr. Steinham? The financials of your organization indicate a steady progression of growth and profit over the last five years and I suspect that your advertising has played a role in that success."

"Well, Miss Boyer, you have certainly done your homework. We have no specific concern with our current arrangement. We simply want to make sure that we are not missing out on contemporary trends of advertising. You represent a company that is fairly new and my research shows that there are a plethora of new representatives in your organization. I was hoping that your firm could inject a fresh look and feel to our business.

And I might add, when I was told that you would be calling on us, I did a little homework myself. I know that you are one of the newer additions to the Ad Agency and I thought that you could bring a totally new perspective to the business."

The exchange continued for more than two hours, each trying to impress the other with facts, figures, and questions. She realized her throat was dry from all the conversation, yet her body was filled with adrenalin. She would not be accused of not keeping up with him.

After the conversation moderated, Mr. Steinham pushed back his chair. "Well, Miss Boyer, you have certainly given me something to think about. With your permission, I would like to introduce you to some of our senior staff. While I will be making the final decision, they will each want to interview and question you over the next few weeks or months."

"Certainly, Mr. Steinham, and please call me Nicki."

"Well then, Nicki, let's get those introductions over with." A large smile came over his face and they settled into a comfortable yet mutually respectful bond.

He escorted her to the other three offices. Mr. Green was an older, pleasant grandfatherly type man, but never offered a smile. She was greeted with, and departed with, a handshake.

Her introduction to the next senior officer was a surprise. "Mrs. Proffit, please meet Miss Boyer." An impressive, tall and immaculately manicured woman stood before her. In a somewhat painful way, she broke a guarded smile. It seemed to suggest that she wanted Nicki to be reminded of her job title. Nicki resisted the need to curtsy.

As they approached the third and final office, Nicki felt the pressure of the day that one feels when overcome by a sense of relief. She stifled the desire to yawn and was glad the day was coming to an end. That's when he walked to the door. As their eyes met, Nicki thought she saw recognition in his gaze. He was the man who took the scat next to her on the plane.

She wondered if he would acknowledge the chance encounter.

Mr. Steinham gave the usual introduction. "Mr. Dixon, this is Miss Boyer. But you'll want to address her as Nicki, as she has generously given us permission to do so."

"That being the case, Nicki, you must feel comfortable calling me Brent."

"Thank you, Brent. I hope we will have the opportunity to work together soon." Right away, she regretted her words. She had not said the same to the other officers yet was reaching out to Brent with some degree of familiarity. Well, they *had* shared a flight.

CHAPTER FIVE

SMILEY - 1944

The stench of bodies surrounded us and bile rose in my throat. We did not have the time to determine if the casualties were ours or the enemy's. We had been ordered to return to one of the previous posts as a small group of Germans had infiltrated one of our earlier battlegrounds. With trepidation, we began to move in. There was no sign of the enemy, but history had told us that if the Germans were good at anything, it was keeping out of sight until the time was right. I decided I would not dispatch reconnaissance around the perimeter, but I knew we needed to draw them out or walk into an ambush.

I called on four of my men to fire into the air, but in various directions. Within seconds, the hostiles began slowly moving in sight, with guns blazing. There was not enough time to acknowledge the terror we all felt. We immediately reacted, utilizing all the training we had been given. The whiz of bullets and clack of weapons being loaded and reloaded ricocheted through my head. I wanted to see the faces of my men, but there was no time to avert my glance. I had to stay focused on the mission at hand.

After a good forty-five minutes, firing ceased but neither side retreated. We soon figured out that the lull was just an opportunity to regroup and gather our breaths. Too soon, the fire was again furious. We hunkered down. We needed back up but there was no time to radio the need. This was our first mission where we did not have the upper hand. I was concerned....very concerned. As the gunfire became more sporadic, cries for help and even dying cries mingled with the sounds of combat. Though I didn't speak German, I understood pleas for help—in both languages. It was sheer agony to be so helpless, but there was no opportunity to attend to medical needs or comfort.

After four strenuous hours, the gunfire slowly died away. Unfortunately, so had many of my men.

CHAPTER SIX

NICKI - 1970

Several months at the Agency had passed. Nicki had gotten to know several of the employees and was beginning to feel like she was really part of the team. She had heard that this industry bred cut-throat business and employee jealousy, but she had not witnessed any of this. There seemed to be cohesion among the staff and she attributed this, in part, to an executive team who was adept at matching client needs with staff skills.

A month after she had visited the client in Dallas, she was summoned to a luncheon meeting with Mr. Dunlap. This would be her first time to lunch in the executive dining room and she was cautiously excited. She arrived ten minutes early, as was her practice. The dining room was quite impressive and had obviously hosted luncheons for clients, for there was seating for at least forty individuals. The artwork on the walls wrapped around a large whiteboard, which would normally have seemed out of place, but it had been mounted with the utmost of professional framing and sat most comfortably among the expensive Remingtons. She envisioned the company executives gathered around the massive central table, each taking turns sketching strategic plans. For a moment, she saw herself in that role, but the image was broken as Mr. Dunlap opened the massive glass door and entered the room.

She was greeted by a smile by Mr. Dunlap. "Nicki, thank you

for joining me and thank you for your punctuality. I've always thought that being punctual was a commendable attribute." She smiled internally. She guessed she had been born with that attribute.

The table was set for two and lunch was brought in. She took a moment to admire the presentation. Each plate held a fillet of braised salmon, surrounded by asparagus and rice. A basket of various crusty breads was placed between the servings and each was provided a small bowl of a seasoned sauce. She would be discreetly watching to see how Mr. Dunlap utilized the mystery sauce. She did not want her rural, small-town background to be obvious.

The lunch proved to be delicious and was punctuated with small talk. She learned that the company had an executive chef, quite the exception, but a tribute to the success of the business. Mr. Dunlap also explained that many business deals had been made at this table and may have been secured, in part, by the stellar meals that had been served. As the plates were cleared, a beautifully prepared salted caramel bread pudding took center stage. She had never seen bread pudding in this preparation, but it was scrumptious. She wondered if this had been served as a homage to her roots, but for whatever reason, she was delighted over it and ate every bite.

Once the last of the dishes had been removed, Mr. Dunlap rolled his chair back and faced her. It was time for business.

"Nicki, what are your feelings on the Dallas account?"

She thought for a minute and said, "Well, Mr. Dunlap, they

were very receptive to my presentation and it appeared to me that they were going to give our agency a favorable opportunity at their account."

He smiled broadly. "Yes, indeed, they were impressed with you, my dear. Mr. Steinham called me within two hours of your visit to their offices and had nothing but good things to say about you. He was impressed that you had done your homework and had a good knowledge of their business." He paused to chuckle. "In fact, it took him a minute or two to even mention our Agency. I had to remind him that YOU represented OUR company."

"Oh, Mr. Dunlap," Nicki said.

"It was never my intention—."

Before she could complete her sentence, it was interrupted by Mr. Dunlap's robust laugh. "Dear girl, I was just getting a rise out of you. You no doubt handled yourself beautifully. You see, you will be the face of our agency. If Mr. Steinham is impressed with you, he will be impressed with the agency."

Nicki breathed a sigh of relief and thought, I could not have orchestrated a better presentation.

"After a suitable amount of time for Mr. Steinham to consider all his proposals, I have now heard from him and he has accepted a contract with our firm. He also made it clear that he would expect you to be the manager for the duration of that term."

It was hard for Nicki to contain her professional decorum. The remainder of their luncheon meeting consisted of Mr Dunlap's plan for her to meet with some of the more Senior Managers so that she would be well prepared for execution of the contract. All suggestions were welcomed and noted on the Planner she had brought with her.

As the two rose from the table, Mr. Dunlap handed her an envelope. "Please accept this little thank you for your successful mission. It is clear to me that I made a good decision when I hired you and I expect great things from you. You have already set the bar very high, my dear."

She graciously accepted the envelope and returned the compliments with appreciation. He followed her to the elevator and she entered, only waiting for the door to close before she exhaled and opened the envelope. She could hardly believe the amount of the bonus and Mr. Dunlap's generosity. It would be a nice deposit to her little nest egg. Soon, her little Corolla would need to be replaced.

***

Brent closed the door to his office. He put aside the folder holding the budget he was reviewing and Mr. Steinham's latest news that The Ad Agency had been selected as the new PR firm and that Nicki would be the lead account manager. Smiling, he thought back to their serendipitous encounter on the plane. He had been disappointed when she showed no sign of interest but had completely understood her reluctance to pursue anything more than the brief interlude. He still was in disbelief at her appearance at his office door.

At their introduction, there had been no sign of recognition on her part. He had been a little disappointed because he thought he had sensed a spark on the plane. Obviously, he had been wrong. His imagination kicked in as he conjured up the possibility of the two working together. He looked forward to the time when he could remind her how they had actually met. Turning his attention back to the budget, he allowed his mind to wander the rest of the day. He hoped for more.

CHAPTER SEVEN

SMILEY - 1944

The air began to clear, but as it did so, my worst fears were confirmed. Dead soldiers covered the ground and the cries for medical attention became clearer. I spotted our medic. A sense of relief came over me that he had not been injured. He dashed from man to man but the demand was overwhelming. By now, I knew enough about war injuries to help, so I began to triage the wounded.

As I made the rounds, I saw familiar faces that wore the last expression they would ever have. I had to put my emotions aside and help to determine who could live another day. I had grabbed some of the triage tags that the medic had made in advance. Time was of the essence. I began to assess and found many who were bleeding profusely, so I was able to apply tourniquets where needed. Once we had evaluated our men and radioed for medical or body transport, I began walking through the bodies and removing one of the duplicate dog tags from each soldier. It had to be done, but it was difficult to keep my emotions in check. Over the months, I had come to know all these men personally. I knew where they were from, their family composition, their hopes, and their fears. When I was trained for this role, I was told it was better to keep a distance, and while I realized the benefit of that, I had no reservations about the intimate and personal relationship I had fostered with the men. It actually helped me to know what role they would play in their service.

I was now saying goodbye to six of them.

The helicopters would soon arrive in the clearing and my thoughts turned to the families back home as they would receive the news of their loved one's death. The devastating news would be delivered by Notification Officers who would convey basically the same narrative to each family. "Your son has fallen at the hands of the enemy. He fought bravely and died gallantly in service to his country. We are sorry for your loss." They would be stoic and impersonal as they handed the mothers a Gold Star Flag, but they would not know these men as I knew them. I did not envy them their thankless job, but I figured they would handle the notifications better than I could have.

The medic and I lined up the men who needed medical attention and followed with the deceased. As I confirmed the total members of my squad, I noticed we were one short. The medic and I dispersed and covered the ground again. After a brief walk, I spotted a rifle appearing to lean against a tree. As I got closer, I saw a shoe and then the military uniform. It was our man. I quickly turned to face him, hoping he needed medical attention but had not been able to cry out.

Then I saw it. The Smile. My entire body seized. It was our Smiley. He had used his last breath to prop himself against the tree, his rifle against him, and he smiled, as if we would be expecting that. A cursory check showed he had sustained a mortal wound to his heart. The wound suggested a trajectory from an elevated position. I glanced out among the trees just as a German was lowering himself from one of them. I took aim but missed and he dashed out of sight.

Tears ran down my cheeks. I knew he was gone, but I checked vitals anyway. I sat down next to him. I put my arm around his shoulders and his head fell to my chest. I felt so guilty. I had hoped to protect him but the battle had consumed the energy of every man, including me. Gathering my composure, I called out to the medic. He, too, was visibly upset when he realized it was our friend and comrade. Together, we placed Smiley with the deceased group and I gently removed one of his dog tags. I silently said a farewell prayer over him. I put my hands in my pocket and felt the folded paper. I had forgotten about it. I didn't take time to look and placed the note with the tag in the hands of the transport officer, asking him to keep the items together. I had taken extra time with Smiley but I figured no one would object. We all had a great affinity for this unique and wonderful soldier.

CHAPTER EIGHT

NICKI - 1970

The postman made his routine delivery at the appointed 10:30 am. He was met, also with regularity, with the wave of Mrs. Boyer, as she watched from the kitchen window. These days, there was not much mail. Since Nicole had a position in Houston, she would send the occasional note, just so they would have something tangible, but most of the time she called. With a pie in the oven, Nicole's mom decided to wait to walk to the mailbox. It was such a pleasant day. She had the kitchen window open, partly because the oven was on, but really, because it was the perfect spring day. Birds would light on the ledge now and then, no doubt tempted by the aroma and were shooed away. She thought that maybe the postman could have enjoyed the sweet smell, if the wind was in the right direction.

She would save him a slice and take it to the mailbox in the morning. Her husband was attending to chores. He knew he could easily get the mail, but he also knew it was one of his wife's great pleasures, so he continued to work in the garden. He was planting for a summer crop, a Victory Garden, and he so enjoyed working with the seedlings and imagining the fruits they would produce in a few months.

Just before lunch, she made her pilgrimage to the mailbox. She gathered the few envelopes and just glanced to see if there was a letter from Nicole, but didn't see anything. She turned her attention to the lunch meal and just before it was to be served, she called out the screen door to her husband.

They sat down at the little table and after the customary blessing of the food, they ate pretty much in silence. Their conversations had whittled down to the mundane things of farm life and doctor visits, and everyday comfort had taken the place of the lively house when Nicole had been home. But they were both very happy for her. They had been concerned that she might not have found a good job after college. There had been little opportunity in the local market and when she had mentioned sending resumes out of state, they reluctantly agreed. She was now settled in what she called a "good position," and they had resolved to share her happiness.

Nicki

Nicki was totally immersed in her work. She was making trips to Dallas on a regular basis. In fact, the people at the airlines began to recognize her and call her by name. She had formed friendships with many of the people at the company, but so far, she had not crossed paths with Brent. Although relieved, she wondered if he even recognized her from their brief encounter months ago.

She was in Dallas when she had received word of a meeting at the home office in Houston. Mr. Dunlap's administrative assistant had called to let her know that her attendance would be required. She was also alerted to the fact that all upper-level executives would also be there.

The notification came just as she exited the elevator to Brent's office.

Knocking on the door, she saw he was on the phone but signaling her to enter.

He concluded the call and looked up at her. "Interesting call," he exclaimed. "That was your Dallas office inviting me to a meeting there."

"Hmmmm," said Nicki. "I just received the same call. It appears that it's for high level staff which makes me very curious."

About that time, Mr. Steinham opened Brent's door. "I understand the three of us need to quickly book a flight to Houston. I'll get Diana to get us on the next plane and arrange a shuttle to the airport."

Within no time, they were arriving at the Ad Agency and entering the conference room, where several seats had already been claimed.

Brent took a chair next to her and Mr. Steinham sat across the massive table. Mr. Dunlap entered the room, looking very business-like.

"Good to see all of you. You might be wondering why I called this meeting. I have an important announcement to make. All eyes were focused on the next sentence. "Well, I am here to let you know that our agency has been named the best agency in the Houston for the year! This has been quite a year. All of you have made major contributions and my thanks to all of you. I hope you won't take exception that I single out one of our newest account executives, though. Nicki Boyer, you have proven to be a great asset to the company and the bottom line. I think we all recognize your talent and the fresh look you have brought to the Agency."

Everyone at the table applauded and smiled their approval of Nicki's efforts. She blushed with delight. There seemed to be a genuine appreciation of her work.

Once the noise died down, Mr. Dunlap spoke again. "Everyone, please stay for lunch, which will be served with one round of champagne. Then, it's back to business for all of us. Steinham, Brent, and Nicki, will you three remain present after lunch? I would like a word with you." All nodded. For Nicki, the rest of lunch was consumed with curiosity.

The room was emptied and the table cleared. Mr. Dunlap broke the silence. "Once again, Nicki, may I commend you on your achievements."

"Yes," Mr. Steinham echoed. "Acquiring your firm for our advertising needs has been one of my best decisions.

You really impressed me with the research you did on our company and how you approached the marketing conversion. We have a couple of sister companies which we considered low hanging fruit, but it occurred to me that you might be interested in helping them stand out."

He directed the conversation to Mr. Dunlap. "Wondered if you might want to let Nicki work with Brent to bring this line of business to light?"

Mr. Dunlap appeared to be thinking. "Nicki, Brent, y'all good with this?"

The two, looking at each other, said almost simultaneously, "Sure."

"Good then. Steinham, why don't we go back to my office and celebrate? I've just gotten a shipment of cigars we can test while Nicki and Brent handle the semantics."

Together, the two men stood and patting each other on the back, took leave of the conference room.

Brent turned to Nicki with a smile. "Well, how about that for a surprise?"

She agreed and wondered if this might be an opportune time to mention their chance meeting on the plane a few months back. Then she decided there would be other occasions. She stood up and formally extended her hand. Brent, thinking a brief hug might have been appropriate, took her hand.

"I'll put together some graphs and forecasts, Nicki, and see you in Dallas soon."

"That will be great. Looking forward to another successful endeavor."

CHAPTER NINE

OLIVER LANGDON – 1945

The gardens were flourishing. I had replanted the vegetable garden and Henrietta was happily enjoying the beauty of her spring flower garden. I had just walked up and down the rows of the vegetables, smiling as I thought of my predecessor. Then, I saw the truck. It was greenish brown in color and held two men dressed in the same hue, seeming to blend right into their surroundings. My first thought was that they were coming to tell us that Smiley was on his way home. That IS what they were telling us, but not as I had thought.

Smiley was gone. The men had served with Smiley. Though it was unusual, they had obtained permission to deliver the news of Smiley's death. They had presented Henrietta with letters of commendation for his marksmanship and a Gold Star Banner for her window. They said he had served his country gallantly. On a personal note, they said he was the most well-liked of any Private they had known. He had walked a thousand miles, always smiling. Units far and wide became familiar with the name, Smiley. Even in death, he was smiling.

I moved closer to Henrietta and put my arm around her waist. I could feel the tenseness of her body. There were no tears. Henrietta had taken the items from the officer and offered a curt thank-you. She turned and walked quietly up the stairs of the porch and into her parlor.

Before the officers turned to walk away, I took the liberty of asking, "Can you tell me more about Smiley's service?"

I corrected myself, "I mean Private Jameson's service."

One of them walked over to the jeep and returned with a folder. Handing it to me, he said, "We brought this along. You are welcome to keep this, Mr. Jameson."

I started to correct his assumption but realized that this was information that would only be given to a family member. I made a choice to remain silent. The two saluted me and walked away.

I maintained my stance as I opened the folder. My eyes quickly reviewed the entries on the paper.

Peter Aaron Jameson, born – 1925

Enlisted in Larkspur, South Carolina – 1944

Physical characteristics – 6'1", 180 lbs, dark hair, dark eyes

Mental limitations noted at time of enlistment

Basic Training Completed in January, 1945

Deployed to France, engaged in several conflicts with Germans

Last battle was in Compiègne, where he had fought admirably.

I was intensely saddened by the news of Smiley's death, but proud of him. The young boy that I always thought would always be a young boy had fooled me.

Smiley had become a young man. Smiley had become a soldier. Smiley had died an honorable death as a man and a soldier.

Two days later, we laid Peter Aaron Jameson to rest next to his father, I did one last thing. Broadly, I SMILED.

What was to happen in the life and death of Smiley would have never entered my mind.

CHAPTER TEN

NICKI AND BRENT

Knowing her schedule was about to get even more hectic, Nicki made a call to the doctor who was listed on her insurance coverage. She was told she could drop by for the follow-up bloodwork at any time. She decided she best get that done before her schedule pre-empted the necessity.

Two weeks later, she was in Brent's office. He was well-prepared. All the material was neatly organized on the work table of his office. She counted the stacks – ten in all. She had tried not to do that but couldn't resist. She didn't mention her eccentricity to him. The coffee pot, accoutrements, and two cups were on the credenza. He poured a cup for each of them, making an assumption that she was a coffee drinker. They began the arduous process of going through the financials of the business. She carefully took notes.

It had not taken much to convince her boss to expand their account to this line of business. In reality, he wasn't really concerned about the type of business or its success. Their role would be in making the business known to the industry. Nicki had proven she was the right person for the job, though there had not been a choice. Mr. Steinham was sold on her value as was Brent. The work was tedious, but Nicki was beginning to understand why the company was being re-examined. There was certainly the potential for revenue. Brent made a call for sandwiches to be brought in and they made quick work of them, getting right back to the business at hand. He was intimately familiar with the business and he was adept in explaining and answering her every question.

When they looked at the clock, it was 7:00 p.m.

"I'm sorry, Nicki," Brent said. "I didn't realize it had gotten so late."

"Neither did I." Her stomach growled, causing her to blush.

Brent straightened the paper on his desk, and turned off the coffee maker. He reached for his jacket. "Will you join me for dinner? I thought I'd stop by the French restaurant on Akard Street. It's some of the best in the city."

Nicki thought about declining but then realized she would have agreed had the offer been made by any other business client. "Sounds good. Just give me a second to freshen up first."

Nicki examined her reflection in the washroom mirror. The image belied her tiredness. She applied fresh lipstick and fluffed her hair. Satisfied, she opened the door with a smile.

Dinner was relaxing and pleasant. A lovely meal, followed by drinks at the nearby piano bar, and neither had required a great deal of conversation. After her second cocktail, she realized the depth of her exhaustion. She suggested that she call a cab to the hotel.

"Don't be silly. I'll be happy to drive you," he insisted.

She watched Brent generously tip the valet and pat him on the back with familiarity, wondering how many women he had brought here before her. He opened her door and she slid into the seat. He began driving to the hotel and she realized he knew where she was staying, but that was just the nature of the business. They were both too tired for mindless conversation and the trip was thankfully, a quick one. He pulled into the circular drive and put the car into park as he started to open his door.

"No," she said. "I appreciate your gesture, but I will get in safely." She turned to him with a smile. "Thank you for the time you allowed me today, the lovely meal and the drinks. I will assemble all the data and send you something to review before I present a formal presentation to the executive staff."

"It was my pleasure, Nicki. I will look forward to the next time. Rest well." And with that, they parted company again.

***

Arriving home after the Dallas trip, Nicki was confident that she and Brent had collaborated well and that she had all the material she needed to pitch the progress to Mr. Dunlap. She wanted to assure him that the Ad Agency was representing a line of business they could easily augment.

She grabbed the mail that had been delivered through the door slot and quickly looked through it. She had received the bloodwork results and opened the envelope quickly. She noticed that the results were the same as before, which struck her as curious. She also saw a pink envelope from her parents.

Stepping out of her heels, she headed for the bath but turned back and picked up the shoes. What was she thinking? She had never left her shoes, or anything, on the floor, and followed her usual routine—clothing neatly placed on hangers, briefcase stowed by the desk, then proceeded to her shower.

Her mind turned back to Brent. By all indications, he had not remembered their brief interlude in the plane. Part of her was relieved, but she also wondered if she had not made the impression on him that she thought. She finished her shower, pulled her gown over her head, and slipped into bed. Thirty minutes later, she still stared at the ceiling. Her head was swimming with numbers, forecasts and graphs. This had never happened before but then, Brent had not been part of the equation before, either.

Arising earlier than usual, but sleep-deprived, she took her much-needed coffee and mail to the sofa and turned on the side-table lamp. Glad to get her parent's letter, she took her time reading it. She missed her parents and longed to see them but there had been so many demands of her time with work, she had been remiss in having a good visit, even over the phone. They seemed to be appealing for a personal visit. She hoped there was nothing wrong at home. They had both been healthy but there was something serious about the letter and in asking her to visit, so she wondered. She would look at her calendar when she arrived at work and try to schedule a three-day weekend soon. All of a sudden, she was homesick.

***

The only difference in her routine this morning was her confident stride. She had her presentation ready and was feeling great about the assembly of the materials. With all her notes converted to a paper presentation, she'd requested an early morning audience with Mr. Dunlap, who wanted to include the other Account Executives. She entered the building, flipping her hair as she greeted the receptionist. The elevator was full of employees, all exiting at various floors and she was then left alone for the last three. She smiled because she was headed to the top. She saw her reflection in the mirrored elevator and she was quite pleased. She was well-rested and well-dressed, the picture of self-assuredness.

The doors opened to the Executive Conference Room and she noticed the coffee was made and there were notepads and company pens at four of the seats. After a quick review, she put a copy of the presentation at each seat.

Content, she poured herself a cup of coffee and waited for the others to arrive. As usual, she had a good fifteen minute wait. She was almost unaware of arriving participants when she realized she had been thinking of Brent. She snapped out of her reverie and extended a good-morning smile to each.

As she had hoped, and even expected, the presentation went well and the outcome favorable. Mr. Dunlap was wearing his "I am proud of you smile," and the other participants followed suit. Once again, she felt lucky that there was no unhealthy competition among her peers. Each success was a success for the others and for the company. She rushed to her office to call Brent.

"Brent, all went well with the program this morning." She chuckled as she said, "I didn't tell them how much progress we had already made on the account. I didn't want to seem presumptuous."

He joined her in the laughter. "So when will you be returning to Dallas?

She thought of her parents' letter. "Oh, Brent, can we wait a week or so? I really need to make a trip back home. My parents are really missing me and I, them."

"Certainly," he exclaimed. "Please take all the time you need. When you return, just give me a call. I will also look forward to hearing about your visit."

As they ended the call, she thought that response had seemed a little personal, but maybe he had just wanted to say something thoughtful about her trip.

Her request for a couple of extra days off was met with approval. In fact, Mr. Dunlap had told her to take as many days off as she needed. She called the airline and booked a flight and then placed a call to her parents. She expected more excitement in her mother's voice when she said she would arrive on Friday, but instead, her words were met with a very somber response. The concern Nicki had earlier was now even greater. Now, she had four days to work before she would be home to learn what was obviously wrong. She decided to bury herself in her work, going over the new account with a fine tooth comb. She spent the four days putting together notes for her next Dallas trip.

***

At 10:30 am, the plane touched down. She had told her parents not to drive over to pick her up, that she would rent a car. The bags were now loaded and the car was in motion. Her mind was racing with thoughts of doom and gloom at home.

She arrived by lunch and honked as she pulled up the narrow caliche road. She could see her father stand, from his position in the garden, a gloved-hand waving. Then, her mother followed from the back door, waving but not smiling. Something was terribly wrong. She could hardly wait to find out.

Superficial greetings were exchanged. There was a feel of tenseness in each move and embrace. Her father took her bags and she put her arm around her mother's waist as they walked toward the house. She thought she could feel her mother trembling.

After lunch, her mother asked, "How about a slice of pie and a cup of coffee?"

She wasn't really in the mood but responded, "Sure, Mother, that would be great."

Dad entered the kitchen, letting her know that her suitcase was in her room. Of course, her suitcase was in her room. Why would he announce the obvious? Was he trying to make some kind of conversation? Nicki had never seen her mom or dad act this way. Strange. Would she face the issue head on or would she just wait a while to see if her parents would broach the subject? Knowing that she was home for three days, she just decided that a later conversation was better. She did not know what kind of news she would be taking back to Houston.

The next couple of days were pleasant but strained. Nicki's anxiety levels were being stretched by the hour. She tried to keep herself busy by taking long walks around the homestead, helping her father in the garden, and even engaging the postman in mindless conversation. She had so looked forward to a homecoming that would be comforting and familiar but this one had proven anything but that.

At Sunday services, the Pastor had spoken of things that test one's character and faith. The words penetrated her heart. Had she unknowingly done something to cause her parents hurt? She wondered if they were just experiencing the empty nest syndrome.

At lunch on the final day of her visit, she watched her mother stir her coffee over and over, her gaze on the floor. Typically, her father would have excused himself to his recliner, where he would read his Sunday devotionals until he dozed off for a nap, but today, he helped his wife clear the table and clean the dishes, even though Nicki had insisted on doing so.

She could feel the anxiety building. At last, the kitchen was back in order and her parents sat down across from her at the table. She finally could not take it anymore. She looked at them head-on.

"OK, y'all, I need to know what's going on here. We have to talk. I will be leaving in a couple of hours and I need to go with a clear head, so please talk to me," she implored.

Her parents exchanged concerned looks and her father began to speak. "Nicki, you know how much we love you, don't you?"

"Of course I do," she replied. "Is one of you sick? Please, please tell me."

Her mother spoke up. "Neither of us is sick, dear, but we are upset with ourselves that we have held information from you, information that we should have shared years ago, as soon as you were old enough to understand it."

Nicki's heart was pounding. What on earth had not been told her?

"You see, Nicki, you are our daughter, but not by birth. We adopted you when you were just an infant."

Nicki grabbed the seat of her chair, fearing she might pass out at this news. She sat there quietly for more than a moment. Her parents were holding hands and they both had eyes full of tears. "Oh, Nicki, please don't be upset with us. Nothing is different, except this knowledge," her father said tearfully.

She began to regain her composure and looked at both of them, seeing the terror in their expressions. "But the knowledge is everything," she exclaimed. "I'm almost twenty-five. Why have you waited this long?"

Her mother spoke. "It wasn't that we didn't want to tell you, dear. It's just that there was never the right time. And then, you were in college and we did not want to disrupt your studies. And now, you've entered a career, and we did not want to alter the path of your success."

Nicki was so confused she didn't know what to ask next. Her parents sensed that, and her father began to tell her how she became their child. "Nicki, in 1945, I was employed by the government to do some reconnaissance work in France. I was stationed at the American Embassy and my work was very sensitive. Your mother and I had been married for just over a year and had found out that we could not have children of our own. We were devastated because we had both wanted a big family. And then I was called to this overseas position, leaving behind a distraught young wife. I spent almost a year in Paris, a separation from your mother that was so difficult on both of us. She went through a very depressive year and I could do nothing to console her.

"As my assignment was coming to an end, I was in a meeting with the ambassador of the consulate and our conversation turned to a personal one. Before I knew it, I was telling him of our situation and the strain I was afraid it would put on our young marriage. It was then that I found out about an orphanage that had recently been constructed. There had been a demand brought on by relationships forged by war, and which had produced an influx of births. He suggested it might be something I could consider. I was intrigued, especially in the knowledge that one of the parents, likely the father, would be of American ancestry. Within days, I found myself at the door of the orphanage. My presence was more than welcomed.

They were struggling to meet the needs of the many new arrivals and seemed anxious to place an infant in my arms. I did not want to rush. I was considering a decision that should have been made by both your mother and me, but I would not be pressured into a hasty conclusion."

Nicki nodded, "That must have been difficult."

"Yes, it was and that being said, I was led into various rooms filled with cribs and mats. There were babies crying in every room and only a few young girls to feed, change, and console them. In the last room I entered, I saw a crib in the back of the room and saw a child who was barely old enough to pull up to the rails. Her bright blue eyes and her curly blonde hair beckoned me. Without hesitation, I walked back to an outstretched hand. With permission, I lifted her from the crib and her hands went around my neck. Her little head was nestled in my neck and my heart was full of love." Her father's eyes filled with tears. "Nicki, that little girl was you. I had gone into that orphanage with an open but cautious mind and I thought if I was to have any interest, it would be in a boy child, but when I took you in my arms, caution and preference melted away."

Nicki realized tears were running down her face. They were also present on her parents' cheeks. "And then what?"

Her mother began. "Your father telegraphed me. Timing was critical and international calls were not available then. The embassy allowed him to telegraph a message. It read something to the effect that he had visited an orphanage and found a child he would like to bring home as ours and would

I consent. It was very impersonal and no more information had been provided, but I decided that's all I needed to know. I immediately went to Western Union and replied, 'Yes, oh, Yes'!"

Her father took back the conversation. He had gotten his wife's reply and had returned to the orphanage to let them know he and his wife had made a decision on the little blonde child. He needed to quickly begin the process of adoption because he was to be sent back home to the States in less than a week. The orphanage let him know that they had expedited adoptions due to the circumstances and would begin the paperwork. It had then occurred to him that he had not inquired into her background. They told him they would provide records when the process was completed. He was allowed another quick visit to his child whose name he had not yet known. She was sleeping so he just stood over her crib and delighted in the knowledge that she would soon be his daughter.

He was thankfully busy preparing all his reports due at his exit so he hadn't much time to think about the future, but he knew that he could hardly wait to get home and begin his new family.

The day had arrived. His bags were in the embassy van and the driver had been directed to take him to the orphanage and wait while he finished the paperwork. He would then drive him and his new daughter to the airport where they would board a government plane with other Americans returning home.

He arrived at the orphanage as, simultaneously, a bus carrying new infants had arrived. His heart fell at the thought of all these displaced children, but the sentiment was soon replaced with anticipation.

He was quickly ushered to the office, where two matronly women waited. The one behind the desk had several papers to be signed and the other would be signing as a witness to the transaction. He was given no time to read the contents, but quickly signed where indicated.

One of the women took a folder from an overflowing file. "This is all the information we have on the child. I hope it helps." With that, she stood and said curtly, "Your child is being brought to you."

"Does she have a name?" he asked."

"She is called Nicole Collette. We do not use last names here for obvious reasons, but there may be something in the file."

Within minutes, the infant was placed in his waiting arms.

She had been bathed and smelled of Castile soap, and a small pink bow had been placed on top of her head. He was quickly ushered out the door, and he assumed they were afraid he would change his mind. He took her small bag of belongings, the most of which were diapers and a bottle, and settled into the van. He was a father. He had no idea how to care for her - when or what to feed her, when to change a diaper, or any of the requisites of fatherhood, but he would learn.

As the plane took to the air, the child began to cry. He had no idea what to do. One of the female passengers asked if she could help. She suggested that the cabin pressure would sometimes affect a child, and she also checked the need for a diaper change.

She asked the baby's name and he said, "Nicole."

The woman began to sing a lullaby and included Nicole's name frequently in the verses. The child began to calm. The trip was long and arduous, but several female passengers stepped in to assist. Thankfully, the plane had milk on board and it was warmed several times for the bottle, the result of which was invariably the need for a diaper change. Supplies were dwindling and he was relieved when the plane touched down. He looked among the crowd on the tarmac and then spotted his wife, Nicole's mother. He dashed to her and they embraced with their baby girl in between them. He handed the child to her and her tears of joy dotted the little blanket wrapped around their baby.

When they arrived home, they were met with a few well-wishers who had brought much-needed baby gifts. By evening, the house was empty, except for the family called Boyer. Mother and father sat in the middle of the bed with the child between them. The baby was beautiful and the couple realized their love for each other and the child was stronger than they could ever imagine.

Several days would pass as parents and child would grow accustomed to one another. A makeshift nursery was tailored and supplies were bought. Schedules were adjusted and life began to take on a greater meaning. They were deliriously happy and the baby seemed to adjust to her new life as well.

The folder he had brought home with him had been forgotten for about two weeks when one day his wife asked, "What did you learn about Nicole's parents?"

He jumped up to retrieve the folder, only then realizing it had very little content. In fact, there was one single sheet of paper upon which the following had been written,

Mother – Duplais

Father – unknown

Birthplace of Child – Paris, France

Birthdate – March, 1945

The mother was obviously French and they presumed the father was American. But there was no time for speculation or questions. After thinking they would be childless, and by Divine Intervention, they were now parents. Their attention was totally focused on the well-being and upbringing of their Nicole.

***

Nicki shifted in her chair. She had not moved, maybe had not even breathed since her father had begun the story of her life. She could not believe her ears. It was one thing to learn she was adopted, but quite the revelation to hear that she was French.

Nicki suddenly had a eureka moment. She recalled the blood test results she had gotten from the two doctors.

"Oh, my gosh!" Nicole almost yelled, "That's it!"

"What is it, dear?"

"My blood type. I had received word that my blood type matched neither of yours. I wanted to mention this to you during this visit, but with this surprise news, I had totally forgotten."

"Yes, Nicole," her father spoke. "Before you had gotten the physical exam, all the results of your bloodwork had come to us. Because we had carefully hidden all this from you, we had made sure you had not seen those results. We knew this would all come to the surface someday."

Nicki sat quietly a while. Both parents exchanged tearful glances and then looked back at her.

"Nicki," her mother said with bowed head. "We are so ashamed that we waited until you had to find out this way. But you surely know how loved you are! We just hope you can forgive us."

Nicki looked at both parents, who seemed to have aged since the three of them sat at the kitchen table. She addressed them, "It's all right, Mom and Dad. I do need some time to process all of this, though. Are my biological parents still living?"

Her father handed her the folder. "This is all we were given, Nicole.

Your biological mother must have given you up soon after she gave birth to you. The only thing provided is her last name. We can only assume that she was French, as you were born in Paris."

Nicki's head was swimming. She stood and began pacing. She needed to get out of the house, but it would soon be time for her to return the rental car to the airport. She could see why they waited until the last minute to tell her the shocking news. In her twenty-five years, she never even suspected this. There were photos of her as an infant, but now, as she thought about it, realized there were none of her at birth. It had never crossed her mind.

"Mom, Dad, as you can imagine, this news has rattled me to my core. I never had any suspicion of being adopted, and I am shocked beyond imagination. I need to get back to my apartment, and analyze all of this. But I want you to know, regardless of the situation and what happens next, you will always be my parents," Nicki said as she hugged them. She could feel their hearts beating against hers as she embraced them together.

The time had come for her to leave, and for that, she was relieved. Against her parent's protests, she left for the airport. Saying good-bye to her parents was emotional and all three cried as she climbed in the car. She hoped she could stay focused on her work when she returned home to Houston. She felt like her life was just beginning.

CHAPTER ELEVEN

NICKI OR NICOLE

She called the office and asked for a couple more days off. What she would do with the time was unknown, but she knew she was not ready to face her work obligations ... or Brent.

For the first time in her adult life, she remained in her robe the following day. The day was spent reading and re-reading the brief information in the folder her father gave her. She pondered on the path her life could have taken had her wonderful parents not chosen her from the hundreds of babies for adoption.

The next day began as any other day, until recently. Actually, the only thing different now was Nicki. She wasn't sure she could give 100% of herself to the work at hand but she had to. The new account would get underway this week. She would be traveling to Dallas in a couple of days.

***

She went through her routine as best she could and before she knew it, she was sitting in Brent's office. He began to ask her about her trip home, how her parents were doing and had she had a good visit. She could not find the words for an appropriate response. In her anxiety, she asked that they dispense with the pleasantries and proceed with the work on the account. Brent looked hurt and apologized that he had been personal, and they moved forward on the presentation she had brought for the new account.

At the end of the day, she was exhausted, but she knew it was not work-related. Her work came easily to her. She had good instincts and her peers and business associates detected that quickly. She was seen as an up and coming Account Executive. She had snapped at Brent a time or two and had offered no reason or excuse. His concerned expression told her he knew something troubled her. In spite of her mental strain, they had made substantial progress on the account.

After work, Brent asked if he could drive her to her hotel. She hesitated, but replied affirmatively. She was noticeably quiet in the car. When they arrived, she politely thanked him for the ride and grabbed the door handle.

"Nicki," he pleaded, "I can tell that something is wrong. I don't want to be presumptuous, but I hope you know that our professional relationship has also become personal, and if I can be of any help…"

She interrupted before he could complete the sentence. "No, no, I'm fine. Thank you again for the ride."

She rushed to her room, almost in tears. She had to get a grip on her emotions. She felt like she had been harsh to Brent and felt a need to apologize.

She made a cup of tea and settled into her chair, folder in hand. She was imagining what her bio parents looked like. Did she look like either of them? Did she inherit any of their genetic traits? Tiredness overtook her and she turned back the bed, confident that tomorrow would be better.

The next day, she was called into Mr. Dunlap's office and provided him an update on the new account. He seemed pleased.

As the conversation wound down, she spoke up. "Mr. Dunlap, I have a request to make. I need a leave of absence. I'm not sure how long I will need to be away, but I would like to begin with a month and the option of more if needed."

"Nicki, I do hope there is not anything involving your health or the health of your family, and I will certainly check the calendar to see if we can spare you, but I want you to entrust me to assist in any way if I can. I do have a little concern since you recently asked for some personal time."

"I know, Mr. Dunlap. I will ask you to trust me that I really need this time, but there is no concern about the health of me or my family."

He opened his planner and marked through some dates and returned to her appeal. "Nicki, take all the time you need. Just let me know after the month if you need the additional time."

"Thank you, Mr. Dunlap." She almost reached out to cover his hand with her own, but said instead, "I cannot tell you how much I appreciate this."

She walked to the door when he said, "Oh, Nicki, before your leave begins, will you be able to attend a luncheon I am putting together tomorrow? It's to acknowledge the kick-off of the new account."

"Certainly, I'll be there. Thanks again, Mr. Dunlap."

Once home, Nicki began researching flight schedules and hotels in Paris. She started a list of what she wanted to do when she arrived. The Ad Agency was so busy. In the last few months, companies had sought out their partnerships. The news of their success had gotten around the industry. She knew, and was humbled, that she had been a part of this success.

***

The business partners had arrived for the luncheon. She had been asked to remain close to the door as they came into the conference room, which had been set with the finest service for lunch. She forced smiles and greetings as they entered, for her thoughts were already in another country. When Brent entered, he leaned forward as though he would kiss her on the cheek, but she maintained a professional stance and he was forced to do likewise. The luncheon went on for hours and perfunctory speeches were made in honor of the major players and successes.

As the participants were leaving, she once again took her role of hostess and accepted their compliments as they exited the room. She realized that the room was now empty, except for her and Brent. He walked over to her and in a professional way, congratulated her on a job well done. She smiled, as she reminded him it was a joint venture. He returned the smile.

He then took her arm and looked at her longingly. "Nicki, I hope I have said or done nothing to offend you.

I will not pretend that I would not like to know you better, and yes, on a personal level. I have felt that way since that first day I saw you, on the plane."

There it was. He did remember their chance meeting on the plane. Her heart skipped a beat. "Brent, you have done nothing inappropriate. I am surprised, though, that you remembered me from the plane. I often wondered if you had. Right now, though, I am not in a place where I would or could consider a personal relationship. I have recently gotten some news that has caused me some great anxiety and will soon be taking a leave of absence so that I might deal with the circumstances."

Brent frowned. "Can I-?"

"Before you ask, it has nothing to do with my health or my parent's health.

It actually has to do with who I am and from where I came."

He held her arm tighter. "Sounds serious. Can I help? I am here for you, Nicki," he spoke softly.

"I appreciate that, but this is something I have to do alone. I am not sure how long I will be away or what my next step will be."

"Then may I ask you to please stay in touch with me?" He handed her a card with his home phone number on it. "Call me anytime and for any reason. You don't have to do this alone." His hand was on her arm and as she placed her hand over his, she felt a warmth spread throughout her body.

"Brent, thank you. I don't know what the future holds but I will try to keep you advised of my status as this journey progresses."

"Good, Nicki, I will count on that. And, if you don't mind my saying, I would like to be a part of that future."

A soft smile covered her face as she looked into his eyes.

As soon as she had gotten home, she called the airline and made reservations. Her flight was three days away. She decided to call her parents with the news. They were subdued. She reassured them that what she was doing had nothing to do with her relationship with them but that she just had to have answers. They accepted her reasoning and asked her to just be careful. She laid out her clothes. Without knowing how long she would be in Paris, she wanted to be prepared, but also pack minimally. She ended up with six outfits that could be interchanged. She had a couple of days without anything to do, so she went over all her work assignments to make sure they were complete and could be covered by one of her peers during her absence.

CHAPTER TWELVE

PARIS

The flight was long and agonizing. The plane was full and she had no privacy. Feeling she couldn't even make notes without them being read by the passenger in the next seat, she tried to sleep. She had decided against making hotel reservations until she got to Paris. She wanted something centrally-located, but to what. She had no idea where she was going or who she was meeting. This was going to be challenging and interesting.

The taxi dropped her off at a hotel near the Champs-Élysées. She thought, if this was a failed mission, at least she could do some sightseeing before she returned home. After unpacking and admiring the beauty of her room, she went to the lobby to pick up a small book of translations. She knew a little French, from the required foreign language she had to take in college, but she was hoping that she would need something with additional vocabulary, so decided it was a good investment.

She inquired at the front desk if there was a library nearby. She would have to take a taxi which the doorman was glad to hail, in return for a tip. Based on his broad smile, she knew she would have to learn more about the money exchange. There was no telling how much she had tipped him.

Once at the library, a magnificent old structure, she made an inquiry at the front desk. She was relieved that one of the attendants spoke some broken English. Nicole explained that she was searching for a family by the name of Duplais, who might have been living in Paris in 1944 or 1945. She was led to an area that housed old telephone directories. There was nothing for either of those years, so she looked in 1943 and 1946. The former yielded nothing and the latter had five listings for that name. Quickly, she wrote each of them down and returned to the attendant. She had listed the addresses as well and inquired as to the locations of each of them. She was given a complimentary map. Three of the listings were fairly close in proximity and the other two were miles apart, on opposite sides of the city.

She returned to her hotel and formulated the questions she would ask if someone answered her calls. All she had was a last name. She was also concerned about the ability to communicate. She took out her book of translations and looked for words and tried to compose sentences such as, I am looking for a woman who would have been around the age of twenty in 1945. All I know is that her last name was Duplais. If she received a favorable response, she would inquire if a baby had been born to the young lady. Would that be too direct? She was at a disadvantage in not knowing much about the French people. She did not want to offend, but how would she get to that question otherwise. If she sensed offense, she would just have to apologize. She made sure she had a translation for that as well.

The first two numbers were no longer in service. On the third call, however, she met with success. The person on the line was elderly and Nicki thought the woman could either not understand her or was hard of hearing. She repeated the question. She was met with a response of several no's, before she could even ask another question. The phone clicked in her ear. After contemplating a call back, she decided to move on to the other two. One of them, she thought, was explaining that they knew no one by that name and it was not their name. She understood the phrase, "wrong number." For the last one, there was no answer. Her hopes were dashed. She would try the last one later, but was not encouraged that there would be a good result. Had this trip to Paris been a waste of time and money?

She was tired, but went to the lobby and purchased a postcard to send to her parents. She kept it brief, telling them she had arrived safely and that Paris was beautiful and hoped she would have an opportunity to see some of the sights. She thought to say that she missed them and closed with, "Love, Nicole." Her parents had never embraced the name, Nicki, which she had taken when she had taken her job. Strangely, now that she was in her birth city, it seemed only fitting that she would refer to herself as Nicole. She grabbed a quick dinner and almost fell into her bed at an early hour. She would awake with a sense of determination, she decided.

Before she knew it, the morning light peeked through the curtains of the room and she jumped up with vigor. She had a headache, surely from the stress of a long flight and the lack of results from yesterday. She grabbed the newspaper which had been slipped under the door. She realized that it was in French, and there was little she could glean from it, but it was interesting nonetheless. She needed coffee.

She dressed and went to the small restaurant in the hotel. The menu was perplexing but with the photos that accompanied the choices, she was able to secure a welcome breakfast. She made a note to ask about the delicate little pastry that accompanied her egg.

Returning to her room, she tried the number for which there had been no answer the day before. It rang several times but just before she was about to disconnect, an elderly woman answered. Nicole asked her the primary question, but was surprised at the response. The woman answered, her French sprinkled with English. "Who is this? Why do you call? What do you want?"

Hesitating, and knowing she was being met with resistance, Nicole changed her introduction. In the pressure of the moment, she said she was just looking for a friend she had met many years ago and did not know how to reach her. The person on the other end of the line could have easily deduced that her voice was not that of one who would have been around twenty in 1945, but apparently, she did not take the time to do the math.

"*Oui*, I know some," she responded.

"Is she there?" Nicole asked nervously. No, no, the caller answered. Move away long ago. Nicole asked for the address but was told it was not known. She wanted to press the woman for more, but did not know what to ask. She would say *au revoir* and wait a day or two before calling again. She relaxed her back. It never occurred to her that she might be on the path of finding her mother this soon. The possibility left her excited and terrified.

The next day, she busied herself by visiting the Louvre, the Eiffel Tower, and the Arc de Triomphe. They were all so beautiful and the history was amazing but with no one to share the ventures, she felt empty. Then, she realized that her birth parents might have been on the very paths she had walked and her sense of pleasure was suddenly restored.

In the evening, Nicki visited a restaurant a few blocks away. When she picked up the menu, again, to find photos, she realized this was done to accommodate the hundreds of tourists to the city. Her advertising skills took charge as she said to herself, "well-played." Her meal was delicious and so different from the evening meals at home, which, by contrast, were so very bland. She noticed that the French incorporated sauces on most of their foods, giving each a dual-flavor. She also realized that she would add some weight very quickly if she remained on this diet long.

On the following day, she tried the number again, waiting until midday. The elderly woman answered again and they each played the roles of the prior call. No progress was made. She was cut off before she could begin a new set of questions. This had to mean something but how would she ever know what.

She had to re-group. These calls had produced only one potential, but dead-ended result. She thought for a moment. Orphanages, that's what I'll look for next. She looked at the list of calls she had made. It would be feasible that someone would seek out an orphanage located close to their home, wouldn't it? Or would they? Perhaps they would try to find one that was nowhere close to where they lived, so that they could put as much distance as possible from their humiliation. She decided to stay with the first scenario. It would mean a return to the library, but what else did she have to do?

The attendant recognized her. Nicki told the librarian that she was now researching orphanages in existence in the mid-1940s. This would be a bit more challenging, she was told, because many of them did not have phones and even some had been opened under the guise of something else, so were unknown. The young lady had Nicole follow her as she traveled through the aisles and aisles of material. They were able to locate two possibilities and during the course of their research, Nicole had shared some of her story. She thought if someone realized the importance of her journey, they might be more receptive, although she sensed that the girl may have already figured out what was happening.

She stopped at a bakery, which were on every corner, and picked up a couple of the little pastries she had enjoyed at breakfast a couple of days before. She learned that they were a blending of croissants and éclairs. As she sat at a sidewalk café, she sipped her coffee and ate her pastry. She allowed herself to soak in the ambiance and culture of the city.

She then tried to call the orphanages. Neither of the numbers worked. Her only hope was to somehow get the elderly woman, who had appeared to know something, to communicate with her.

She would take a taxi to the address tomorrow.

It was still early in the day and, although she could take in more of Paris, her mind was so fixed on the mission at hand, she was not motivated to explore. She wandered through the lobby of the hotel and once again, stopped at the postcard selections. She picked out one of the Eiffel Tower at dark. It was so beautiful. She must take the time to visit again, but when it was a bright tower against a dark sky. She sat down in the lobby and took out a pen, and addressed the card to Brent. It was not what she intended, but it was done before she knew it. What would she tell him? She decided on the truth. Very succinctly, she explained why she was there. She wondered if he would feel differently about her. She signed her name as Nicole. This is who she was. It was who she was all along.

She asked the taxi driver to stop at a bakery on the way to their destination. She picked up a beautifully decorated single-layered cake. Perhaps she should have gotten wine instead. They drove up a hill, surrounded on either side by terraced vineyards. As he pulled up to the chateau, she was overwhelmed with the beautiful flower gardens around the entrance. She asked him to wait until she signaled him off.

She knocked at the door. She could hear movement inside but no one answered. She knocked louder. In a moment, the door creaked open and a less than friendly face greeted her. She began to speak, using the same rhetoric as before. She tried to hand the cake to the woman, who refused it. Without some command of the French language, Nicole was helpless.

The woman was nervous and uninviting, and there was nothing left to do but turn away. Nicole had played her last card. She returned to the taxi and when they reached the hotel, she handed the toll and the cake to the driver, who was most appreciative.

It was time to assess the trip, Nicole thought. She had arrived with a last name and not much else and had exhausted that lead. She was depressed at the thought of returning home without any results but it appeared to be the only thing to do.

She spent the next few days doing what tourists would do. She had decided that, if she was to be here, she may as well learn something of her birthplace. Each attraction was more impressive than the last and she had concluded as she closed in on the week that she would return home. Before she made an airline reservation, she decided on one more trip to the library. If there was nothing more for her there, she could at least extend her appreciation to the attendant who had been so helpful.

The next morning, she hailed a taxi and arrived at the library at 10:00, just as they opened. The attendant was not at the desk so she ambled between the aisles, as though some significant lead would jump into her hands. As she was about to leave, she spotted the attendant upstairs, assisting another patron. The young lady waved and signaled that she would be down shortly. Nicole took a chair and waited.

Within minutes the young lady was standing before her, and with an animated voice, said, "Thank you for returning. I have something for you." She went to her desk, pulled out a piece of paper, and handed it to Nicole. "It probably won't help, but I was explaining your situation to my aunt, and she wrote this down for you. I have tried to translate to your satisfaction."

Nicole held the paper in shaking hands. It held a paragraph written in French with an English translation underneath, and it said: *There was an orphanage on Le Boulevard that I remember. It was overflowing with French/American babies in need of homes.* The paper also listed an address.

A surge of hope brought a smile to Nicole's face. "Oh, it is more than to my satisfaction. Thank you so much, and please, thank your aunt. I was about to return home, thinking I had exhausted all leads, but this gives me new hope." With that, she gave the young girl a kiss on each cheek and left the library.

Without hesitation, Nicole directed the taxi driver to the address on the paper. He pulled up to a dark and foreboding building, which appeared to have been empty for years. Of course, what had she expected, an orphanage still in existence after twenty-five years? She had the driver wait at the curb as she approached the building. It was indeed empty, but she noticed a small placard in the corner of the window. It read, "New location at Elise Station." The card was worn and faded so there was little chance the new site was still in use, but she was taking no chances. She relayed the new address, and he headed across town.

The name of the building was Children Services. Her heart was pounding. She entered the door and saw a receptionist. Nicole asked if she spoke English. She shook her head no, but held up a finger signaling Nicole to wait. She returned with an older woman who spoke English fluently.

"Is this an orphanage?" Nicole asked.

"No, dear, this is a clinic for children who have a sickness."

Nicole lowered her head. Sensing her disappointment, the woman asked, "What are you in need of? "

"I am looking for adoption records. I had visited the prior location and the sign in the window directed me here."

The woman put her hand on Nicole's. "Dear, maybe I can help you. The orphanage you seek is no longer present, but it was at this location until it closed. Our clinic purchased the building from them and with that, all their records, which we keep in the level below our main building. We have had no interest in them in years and we have, in fact, scheduled a destruction of all the records within the week."

Nicole could not believe the timing. Of course, she still didn't know if this was the orphanage she was looking for, but this was her first big lead.

"Oh, please, may I examine the records before they are destroyed?" Nicole begged.

She went on to explain why she was interested. The woman, who had now introduced herself as Genevieve, told Nicole it would be most out of the ordinary, but she assumed since the records were scheduled for destruction, there would be no harm. She asked her to return the following day at 3:30 pm, as the office would be closing shortly thereafter, and there would be no prying eyes. Nicole was delirious. She hugged Genevieve and rushed to the taxi.

There was no sleep that night. Even so, Nicole arose at the regular time and spent a good two hours in the hotel gym, just to pass the time. She arrived at the clinic at 3:20. Genevieve was waiting at the desk for her, key in hand. She clicked on a flashlight and led Nicole down a dark flight of stairs.

“Sorry, no electricity down here.” Genevieve aimed the flashlight at a dusty cabinet wedged into a corner. “The records are in there.” She handed the flashlight to Nicole and excused herself.

Undaunted, Nicole began opening the drawers of the cabinet, carefully going through each folder. It was difficult and time consuming and seemed fruitless, when … she spotted the name Duplais. With her heart pounding out of her chest, she pulled out the folder. She quickly removed the single sheet.

Her eyes could not read fast enough.

Isabella Duplais, Mère

Nicole Collette, bébé

Les deux sains

Bébé porté à terme

Mère donne des droits à l'orphelinat

note de bas de page: La mère revient dans un mois pour vérifier bébé, dit de l'aviser à son adresse si elle est nécessaire, mais elle ne sera pas en mesure de s'occuper de l'enfant

Nicole sat on the dust-covered floor, paper in hand. She began to sob uncontrollably. Recognizing the name Duplais was enough. She knew she had found her birth record. She would write this down and translate when she returned to the hotel. Genevieve found her there an hour later, as she arrived to tell her the clinic was closing. She helped Nicole to her feet and led her to the door. Nicole had no recollection of what she said to thank her but she realized later that Genevieve had folded the paper and tucked it into Nicole's handbag.

***

Nicole returned to the hotel. She was a combination of nerves, anxiety, and exhaustion. She smiled when she discovered the record that Genevieve had put in her handbag. There was no question of her maternal roots.

She said her name aloud. Nicole Collette Duplais. With the help of her translation book, she determined that she had been carried to full term, both she and her mother were healthy, and her mother gave her rights to the orphanage. It seemed her mother had also returned in the following month to check on her child. The speed with which all of this was happening was beyond her wildest dreams. She reviewed the information again, and realized the address her mother had provided the orphanage was the same one she had visited and been turned away. Her heart pounded. Could the woman who would not see her be her mother? She knew what had to be done, and this time, there would be no shutting the door in her face.

Nicole reached toward the phone and was tempted to call right away, but thought that re-visiting in person would be much more effective. The red light on the phone blinked, signaling a message. She called the main desk and was told that she had missed a call from a gentleman by the name of Brent Dixon. She had all but forgotten the postcard she had mailed a few days ago. She calculated that it would have been 2:00 am in the States when he had called. Just knowing that made her think more of him. She knew that she had been less than cordial with him recently, but she had been so preoccupied with her assignment that she had not taken the time for pleasantries. Now, of course, she realized that there was something more than a business relationship between them and she was pleased. It was about time that something in her life was stable. But she would address that later. Right now, she was in the throes of matching mother to daughter.

The next day, a taxi was waiting at the hotel and by luck, it was the same driver who had taken her to the address on the paper. He remembered Nicole from a previous trip so knew immediately where he was going. The scenery was now familiar as was the walk to the door, but the last time she made that walk, she had no knowledge of who would be opening it. This time, she was quite sure it was her mother.

She took the steps slowly and reaching the threshold, knocked softly before remembering it took a more deliberate knock to get the woman's attention. When she rapped harder, the door opened. At first, no words were exchanged.

The woman squinted. *"Pourquoi es-tu revenue?"*

Nicole recognized the word 'why.' "I think you know," she replied. "May I come in?"

The woman stepped aside but still wore a scowl on her face as she motioned her inside.

Nicole looked into the woman's face and thought she saw some of her own features. Nicole walked past her, looking at the scarce décor of the room. It was unkempt. Dust covered picture frames and knick knacks. She took a chair and pulled out the sheet of paper, deciding it best to be direct. Her hand shook as she handed it to the woman, who studied it as she sank into a chair.

Nicole looked straight into her eyes, asking, "Are you Isabella?"

The woman did not answer and looked away.

Nicole trudged on. "Are you the woman who took an infant to an orphanage in 1945?"

Now the woman examined Nicole's face. Nicole realized that she was looking for shared features just as Nicole had done earlier.

"What is your name?" the woman asked.

"My name is Nicole Collette." The woman put her hands to her face. She remained silent for several minutes.

The woman lifted her gaze to Nicole's face. "I cannot say I am not the woman. This was many years ago. I was a young girl. Soldiers everywhere and we girls lonely." Her English was limited, but Nicole could grasp what she was saying. "One night, young boy, we were foolish. He say name is Smiley. He was new at *amour*. I took him to my room, showed him. He was frightened. Left soon." She shook her head. "Two months go by and I know I have *bébé* and not ready to be a *mère*. I had no husband, no support." The woman sighed and clasped her hands in her lap. "Yes, I gave *bébé* to orphanage. You....that *bébé*." She bowed her head and sobbed.

Nicole walked over and put her arm around Isabella's shoulder. She sensed the years of distress her mother had endured. Then, she began to cry softly as well. The woman told her that many years later, she married, and went to the orphanage for the child, but she was gone, and they would tell her nothing of what happened to her.

Now that Nicole had found her birth mother, she wasn't sure what would happen next. She decided to share what her father had told her with the woman. Communication between them was difficult and Nicole had to refer to her translation book several times, but the woman, her mother, was nodding her head in acknowledgment, so Nicole could only assume that she understood. The woman told her she never had other children and that her husband had died several years ago.

Nicole wanted to tell her more.

"I have a family," she said, "a wonderful mother and father, in the States. I just recently found out about my history and simply wanted to see if I could find you. I have done that and I hope that you are all right with that. I do not want to burden your life and I may not ever see you again when I leave Paris, so thank you for seeing me, for meeting me."

Isabella stood and went to the kitchen. Nicole, a little puzzled, returned to her chair. The woman returned with two glasses of wine, offering one to Nicole. She held up her glass and said, "To Nicole." Nicole held hers up as well as the glasses clinked. They sipped their wine in silence.

Nicole stood. "Well, I guess it's time for me to go." The perfect words were not coming to her. She had just found the woman who had given birth to her 25 years ago. "May I ask your age, Isabella?"

"*Oui*, I am forty-seven." Nicole was shocked. She looked much older.

Isabella saw Nicole's reaction and frowned. "I am not well."

Nicole dared not ask what was wrong, but told her she was sorry. "May I write to you or call you, Isabella?" The woman nodded her head affirmatively, but in truth, Nicole wished she hadn't asked. What would they talk about after this tense meeting? At least, they each knew the truth and there was comfort in that. They exchanged an uncomfortable hug and Nicole walked down the steps to the taxi. She looked back to see Isabella glancing out a window, with a frail hand in the air. And just like that…mission accomplished.

***

Upon Nicole's return to the hotel, she called Brent.

A sleepy voice answered, "Hello?"

"Brent, it's Nicki. I found my mother."

His voice awoke. "What? Already? I expected it to be more challenging."

"At first, it was. I was really facing dead ends. Then, something very surprising happened. I will tell you all about it later."

"And what did your adoptive parents say?"

Startled by the question, she realized she had not called them first. "Oh, I'm about to call them now." She was sure he was smiling that he had been called first.

"Nicki, thank you for calling me. I am anxious for you to get home and share all the details."

"I will, Brent, and thank you for being there." Suddenly, she realized the significance of Brent in her life.

Nicki did not want to call her parents at that moment. First, it was the middle of night there and secondly, how would she convey the news? She wanted to be careful that she did not hurt their feelings. She just decided she would wait until she was home. She called the airline and booked a flight.

It wasn't until she was on the plane that she began to relive the conversation with Isabella. Her father, young, new at love, and the name Smiley. None of that, except the young part, squared with being a soldier. Since her leave of absence had not taken the time expected, she would use the remaining time to find out about the man named Smiley, who was her father. She immediately wondered about his name, for she knew that his given name was Peter. She was now eager to learn more.

CHAPTER THIRTEEN

HOME

Arriving home, Nicole took a couple of days to unpack and organize everything she had taken with her. She then called her parents, making sure the tone of her voice was not one of excitement. They had taken the news graciously, as she knew they would. They didn't ask too much about the trip nor the visit with Isabella and she didn't volunteer. Thinking back, there weren't too many revelations anyway.

She then called Brent. "Brent, this is Nicole."

"Nicole?" he questioned.

"I guess it sounds strange, but after being in Paris and seeing my birth information, it just seems that Nicole suits me more."

"Well, Nicole, I am glad you are home and that it was a productive trip."

"Yes, and I was able to see some of the beautiful tourist spots as well. Paris is a beautiful city. You know, it's called the City of Light and Love."

"Sounds like I need to schedule a visit someday, maybe with someone I care about."

Nicole smiled into the phone. She couldn't help but wonder what it would be like to explore that romantic city with Brent.

"By the way, Nicole, your account is performing very well. Will you be returning to work soon?"

It occurred to her that she had not given one thought to work since her arrival in Paris.

"I'm glad to hear that everything's going well at work because I'm not quite ready to come back. I need to learn more about my father, who was called Smiley. All I know is that he was a young American soldier and Isabella, my Parisian mother, told me he was young at love and I am not exactly sure what she meant by that."

"Interesting," Brent said. "Call me anytime during your trip. I know you need to close that chapter, but I will miss you."

***

Nicole knew she had sketchy information about her father, at best, but had to start somewhere. She looked up the number of the local Army recruiters, called, and was given a different number for accessing military records from World War II. A young man answered with a formal tone.

She identified herself, "Hello, this is Nicole Boyer and I am trying to get some information on my father."

"Living or deceased, ma'am?"

"Deceased," she said with a shiver.

"Serial number, please."

"I'm afraid I don't have that kind of information, sir. You see, he was my biological father and I was adopted. I'm trying to find out about him."

"Well, what do you know, ma'am? We have hundreds of thousands of records."

Nicki realized it would likely be impossible to find someone with just the name Smiley. "Well," she said, "I know very little. He was in World War II and was serving in France until his death in 1945. His name was Smiley but I suspect that was a nickname."

His voice became brisk, "Ma'am, do you really think that we could locate a soldier with only that information?"

She could tell he was annoyed, but she was desperate. "Oh, I think he may have had limited mental capacity."

"Yes ma'am. Some did when they went in and some did when they got out. I really don't think I can help you. Do you even know he was in the Army?"

"I don't, but in those days, that was the branch of the military where most enlisted." Her voice cracked. "Sir, I know you don't have time for me but I have just recently found out that I am adopted and I am desperate to find my father." She began to sob.

Sensing her urgency, the young man thought a minute. "Ma'am, if you can give me a couple of days, I'll make some inquiries. I know we have been working on a database of World War II veterans and I will look into that, though I don't think the project has been completed."

Nicole closed her eyes and said a little prayer.

"Call me in two days. Name is PFC Ferguson, ma'am."

"Thank you so much. I know this is probably out of the scope of your duty, but I appreciate you so much."

***

After a very long two days, Nicole called the officer.

"Officer Ferguson, this is Nicole Boyer. You asked me to call you today, regarding the information on my father."

"Oh, yes, Miss Boyer, I did. I don't know if what I have here is of much use to you, but I actually found a 'Smiley' in our records. It took some doing and looks like this is the enlistment name. Smiley Jameson, born 1925, enlisted in Larkspur, South Carolina. The death date was not populated on the preliminary database. These are early transcriptions and keep in mind that all our records are in the process of being compared to more current data. This particular entry has not been updated. Sorry, that's all I can find."

Nicole was excited. "That's more than I ever expected, Officer. Even if it turns out not to be him, it's something. I am indebted to you."

"At your service, Miss Boyer, and good luck."

With that, Nicole fell back into her chair and closed her eyes. Silently, she said to herself, "Oh, please let that be him."

CHAPTER FOURTEEN

NICOLE 'MEETS' SMILEY

She had decided to fly to her parents' home, rent a car, and drive to Larkspur, South Carolina. Once again, Nicole found herself in the air. She was glad this trip would afford another visit with her parents. She felt like she could reassure them with her presence. She would tell them of her new discovery, which was not a guarantee. She rented a car and had a pleasant drive home, where she was met with open arms. Their visit was more comfortable than the last one and they reassured her that they understood her desire to know of her biological parents.

After a full day and sleepless night, Nicole headed down the state highway, her route to South Carolina planned the night before. She contemplated what she might be able to discover about Smiley once she arrived in Larkspur. After five hours of driving, Nicole followed county roads to a small town that looked like it was deserted. As she drove down the main street, the only sign of life was an old mutt, looking for food. A flashing marquee reading Vacancy caught her attention and she pulled into the broken concrete drive of the small, old motel. Although it showed signs of better days, she was grateful to find it. She was led to a small but clean room, all she really needed.

The following day, Nicole rose early. There was no coffee pot in the room so she walked to the office, where the clerk looked up from her magazine.

"Do you, by chance, have coffee?" Nicole asked, as she stifled a yawn.

The clerk shook her head. "Nope, but the diner up the street will have it. You can't miss it. It's the only one in town." She abruptly returned to her magazine.

Nicole decided to walk. It was a brisk morning and she had dressed comfortably for the trip. It felt good to get some physical exercise.

A bell rang overhead as she opened the door. The diner's lone customer looked up from his scrambled eggs, nodded and smiled, and returned to his meal. She grabbed a paper from the news stand and took a seat at the counter. The waitress walked right over, placed a mug before her, and poured coffee. Nicole was not sure how the woman knew it was what she wanted, but she smiled at the intuition. She enjoyed the leisure and the charm of the vintage diner. Smiley must have loved it here, she thought.

More customers began to come in. She surveyed the booths, almost all full. This must be the place where locals congregated. Then, she realized, it might be a perfect venue to obtain some information.

She directed her question to the waitress. "Pardon me, but are you familiar with someone who lived here called *Smiley*?"

"No, can't say I am, sugar. Do you know when he lived here?"

"About 1944," Nicki answered, immediately realizing that the waitress was many years her junior, so of course, she would not know of him.

With a giggle, the waitress confirmed, as she said, "I'll be glad to ask some of the old timers, though, if you want."

"Yes, please." Nicki took a napkin and wrote the phone number of the Sleep Well Motel, along with her name. She pondered on writing Nicole Collette Jameson, but thought better of it. She chuckled under her breath. Paris was a far cry from this. Smiley must have thought so, too.

After breakfast, she took a walk through town. Most of the storefronts had closed long ago, but the post office and town hall remained busy. She entered each, asking if anyone had knowledge of her person of interest. There was no indication of familiarity. For all she knew, Smiley had not lived but enlisted here.

She picked up a map, but realized it was for a nearby town, which was more populated. She returned to her room, with nothing to do but watch the one fuzzy-pictured channel on TV. She woke up at dusk, not realizing she had dozed. She must have been more tired than she had thought.

Her stomach told her it was dinner time and she headed back to the only diner in town. The menu offered nothing particularly healthy so she just opted for the chicken-fried steak. As one would expect, it was delicious She took her time, knowing there was nothing else to do in town or at the motel. She eavesdropped on the conversations around her, never knowing if someone would drop a name that would help. Finally, she took the familiar path to the Sleep Well. She hoped she would…

Another day, another cup of coffee. She was not sure how many more days she would invest in a community that was not yielding any clues of her Smiley. She walked over to the library. There were probably less than a hundred books on the shelves, but she spotted a shelf with old newspapers. She walked to the front desk, asking the now familiar question about her Smiley. The librarian said they had no reference material, but pointed to the newspapers Nicole had observed. She said that one of their town pioneers had recently died and a family member had brought the papers to the library. Hoping to find an obituary or an article about local servicemen in the war, she quickly went through them, finding nothing of interest. Disillusioned, she returned to the motel.

She had just sat on the side of the bed when the phone rang. "This the girl looking for Smiley?" the male voice asked.

Her voice quavered. "Yes, Yes, it is."

"Well, lady, ole Smiley is long gone from here, he done be killed in the war. He ain't got no family living, either. But you might try the old hermit, Oliver Langdon. He was a good friend to the family. I ain't seem him in a crow's age, but I think he's still living in the old shack down by the crick. Good luck to ya, now, you hear?" And with that, he was gone. He had never identified himself and she hadn't the time to ask, but she now had some hope.

The next day, as she sat at her now regular spot at the counter, she began to ask around to see if anyone knew of Mr. Langdon. One of the older men in the corner mentioned she should check the whittlers at the gin, who might know of him. She had totally missed that old building, so hastened over as soon as breakfast was completed. She approached, and took in the view. Five old men were gathered on the weathered planks of the front of the cotton gin and each were whittling and spitting alternately.

She approached, but kept her distance, given the direction of the spittle.

"Gentlemen," she spoke loudly, "Do any of you know the whereabouts of Mr. Langdon, Oliver Langdon? I'm told that he lives near a creek."

They all began speaking at once so she focused on the response from only one. A voice projected out of a mouth that seemingly held no teeth. "Young 'un, you need to turn around and follow that road down to the fork and take the one on the right. Go about, oh, I dunno, a mile or so and you can't miss that ole place. That's where the sheriff lived back in the day and ole man Langdon moved into it after Smiley's mother passed on."

Smiley's mother! She was beginning to feel like she may have hit the jackpot.

Not wanting to miss a moment and with nothing else to do, she thanked the men and began to walk in the suggested direction. After taking the right fork in the road, she found herself on a narrow path in a forest.

The weather had turned chilly, the sun being masked by the canopies of the trees. It was also dark. She shivered, but was determined to keep walking.

Several minutes had passed when Nicole spotted a cabin, a shack, really. It had to be the place. She quickened her pace. A beautiful vegetable garden stretched along the side of the property. She guessed that the occupant lived off the land. She approached the residence with trepidation. The steps creaked as she walked up to the uneven wooden porch. Her heart raced. Would she be met with the barrel of a shotgun? She raised her hand and knocked. There was no answer. She saw a small window at the side of the door and after knocking a second time, she stepped aside and peeked in. She could see nothing except some tired, old furnishings.

She jumped at the sound of a rough male voice behind her. "Who are you and what do you want?"

She held up her hands, as though she had been caught breaking the law. "Sir, I mean no trouble. My name is Nicole Boyer and I am looking for Oliver Langdon."

"That's me. What do you want from me?"

"Nothing more than information, sir." Her voice shook. "I am told that you may have known a man who may have been my father."

The man pursed his lips. "Who would that be, then?"

"All I know is that he went by Smiley. I am not sure if that was his given name or a nickname."

Nicole saw his expression of surprise.

"Couldn't be your father, girl. He had no wife. No children."

"But, sir, if I could just have a moment of your time...I have a story to share with you."

The elderly man walked past her and opened the door of the cabin. She stood at the threshold a moment until he signaled her inside. He went to the kitchen and made them both a cup of coffee. She took a sip and felt the warmth return to her body, which was cold from the walk, and the fear.

Mr. Langdon sank into a shabby recliner and gestured toward a sagging couch. "Have a seat." When Nicole complied, he said, "Now, what is this story you want to tell me?"

Nicole began to communicate the saga, hoping she revealed enough detail to convince the man of her legitimacy. He grabbed a pipe and took some time with the ritual of preparing it for smoking. Soon the cabin filled with sweet smelling smoke.

"That's an interesting story, young lady." Without another word, he pushed himself up from the recliner, went over to a shelf, and retrieved a book. Opening it, he took out a folder and an envelope and handed them to Nicole. He set aside his coffee cup and watched her face as she opened the folder and read its contents. She studied it for a while.

As she opened the envelope, a dog tag fell into her lap. She picked it up and examined it, then clutched it to her chest. Was this the first tangible item of her father's existence?

She reached back into the envelope, removing a folded sepia-toned note.

"I have no idea what it says but you can have it," he said quietly.

Le garçon nommé Smiley était gentil mais effrayé. J'étais gentil avec lui. J'espère qu'il survivra à cette *guerre*.

Since her trip to France, Nicole's knowledge of the French language had improved. She read slowly and could make out something about boy named Smiley, being scared, and hoping he would survive battle.

When she had finished reading it, she dropped the note into her lap, and looked up. "Mr. Langdon, I believe if I read this correctly, it may have confirmed my story, that Smiley was indeed my father. Do you know who wrote this note?"

"Girl, when ole Smiley went on, the tag and note were delivered to his mama. The officers who delivered these gave me the folder. They didn't bother to tell her the circumstances around that. Smiley's mother didn't know what to make of this note but I was curious, so I found out who his platoon leader was and wrote to him. I had a phone back then and I was surprised to get a call from him one day. He explained all about his platoon and their visit to Paris one evening. He said the lady friend of your Pappy gave him this note the morning after." The old man turned away, visibly uncomfortable.

He left Nicole to her thoughts and returned to the kitchen to refill their cups.

"Girl, I don't know how much you know of your Pap, but his commander told me all about Smiley's basic training, his marksmanship skills, and his ability to fight. He also said his fellow officers were very affectionate toward him." Her heart was full, knowing how well he was thought of.

"Mr. Langdon," she appealed, "please tell me your personal remembrances of my father."

He hesitated before speaking. "I guess you are Smiley's daughter. I can see the resemblance. You know that he never knew about you. He wouldn't have understood."

Not entirely sure of what he meant, she implored, "Please continue."

He began to tell her of Smiley's early life, his parents, and his patterns of behavior. She sat on the edge of her chair, absorbing every word. With the details of his obsession with numbers and habits, her interest was piqued. She saw some of those very attributes in herself. He told her of Smiley's desire to enlist and how he had been sure that he would be rejected once they realized he was not "normal," but to his surprise, he not only performed at an exemplary level in training camp, he was sent to France to fight against the Germans, where again, by all accounts, he had done a fine job. The call from Smiley's commander had confirmed that as well.

Nicole was proud, but as she intently listened to every word, especially that word "normal," she began to realize something about her father. She believed that he may have been autistic, a condition that had only been identified in the last few years.

She mentioned her theory to the old man, who didn't quite understand the terminology, but acknowledged that Smiley had some of the same characteristics.

"Girl, do you want to see where he and his family lived and where they are buried?"

"I would be so appreciative, Mr. Langdon."

"Meet me in town tomorrow. Where are you staying?" he asked, as if there had been options.

"I am at the Sleep Well Motel, Room 106," she replied.

He stood, ushering her to the door. "I will be there at 10:00 sharp, girl."

"That will be fine, Mr. Langdon. I shall be ready at 9:45."

Their discourse had ended. The door closed before she could walk down the steps. Evidently, Mr. Langdon must not have been too concerned about her ability to make the trek back to town. The forest was even darker than before and she shivered as she increased her pace. She admitted to herself that she was a little frightened, but she continued to move forward, counting her steps as she pursued the same course.

The night seemed much longer than usual. Nicole's anxiety was heightened as she thought of the prospect of visiting her father's home and burial site. She woke early, walked to the diner, and returned with some sausage biscuits and coffee for both herself and Mr. Langdon. As she approached her room, she spotted the bent figure walking up and glanced at her watch. It was promptly 10:00. She handed him a coffee and was met with a gruff thanks.

He said little, but began walking and she obediently followed. After a brief and brisk walk, they came upon a small home surrounded by a short iron fence. The gate was ajar and he moved it out of the way to let her enter first. She took a moment to study the worn structure. Although the walls had weathered to a faded gray and weeds grew as tall as the dingy windows, she could almost picture the home with a frame of beautiful wildflowers around it and honeysuckle hugging the fence. He asked her to wait while he went inside, just to make sure no varmints were making home there. A hand out the door gestured her forward.

She entered cautiously, as though she was intruding on the occupants. He was silent as he moved around the house. She took more time, soaking in her history. The house was furnished and it appeared that it had been untouched since the last occupant took leave. There was a cup on the coffee table. She wondered who had last sipped from it. The kitchen cabinets were full of supplies, though it seemed some had been ransacked.

"Animals," he murmured.

A small bath, with only a tub, separated the two bedrooms at the back of the structure. She walked into the smaller of the two. Opening a small closet, she found a few shirts and pairs of overalls. She pulled them toward her, as if to smell them This had to be her father's room, she thought. The walls were bare. She supposed, given his personality, that he had no collections or real outside interests.

She walked across the bath to the other room. It looked like it was warm and inviting at one time. A worn quilt, its squares in hues of red, blue, and yellow, still covered the bed, but what caught her attention were two framed photographs on the wall. One, a couple, with a young boy, the couple looking older than one would expect to see with such a youth. The other photograph was a young man, wearing a uniform. Chills raced through her veins. She knew that she was looking at her father. She moved in closer and touched the image, tracing the subject with her finger. She studied his face. She saw her eyes in his.

The old man walked to the bedroom door and watched her for a moment. Finally, he spoke. "Girl, that's your pa, Smiley. We never saw him with the uniform, but when the letter came to me, the photograph had been sent to his mother. It was her proudest moment."

Nicole smiled. She could just imagine the pride his mother had as she placed the photograph in the frame and on the wall. She moved over to the other photograph. "Were these…"

"Those were the parents, girl, with their boy. They sure loved him. They never thought they would have children and they were thrilled when he came along. They never saw his differences, or if they did, they never said so. They never even had a question about his strange habits." He paused as if pondering his next words. "Maybe that's the way Our Maker intended. He gave them a son that they saw as just about perfect. They loved him with the good and the bad. I was their neighbor back then. Guess you could say I took him under my wing, tried to make something out of him, and then I helped out when his pap left the earth. When his mama died, she left me this place. Too many memories. I just left and moved down to the crick. I've been by to check on it a few times, but have no use for it. Guess it will just return to the earth."

She blinked back tears. She turned to look at the photographs again. She was looking at her father and her grandparents. She had an overwhelming desire to talk to them, to let them know who she was.

"Take them if you want them," he said. "In fact, take anything you want. I have no use for any of it. Won't be long until I am joining them." He walked over and lifted the photos from the wall. Dust flew as he ran his hand along the edges to remove what was left. "We'll put them on the porch and pick them up after we go to the cemetery."

She had almost forgotten the second part of the visit. They walked out the door. She noticed two depressions in the yard, on either side of the broken sidewalk.

He moved to her side and spoke. "This here was the flower garden and it was his mama's pride until his pap died." He pointed to the other depression. "Over here was the vegetable garden. This is where Smiley walked. He walked up and down the rows of vegetables. I guess he was counting as he walked. He was pretty keen on his numbers."

She tried to envision the small boy in the photograph, as he walked and counted along the rows. The ground was now covered with thistles and weeds.

Time waits for no one, she thought.

Leaving the gate, they proceeded down what was apparently a
rock path at one time. For the most part, it was covered with
moss and weeds with the rock little more than a memory.
They walked up a hill. In the short distance, she could see an
area that had been enclosed with a rock wall. A small
opening served as an entrance. They entered, only to find
three small headstones surrounded by brush and weeds.
They walked over and pulled back the overgrowth to reveal
the headstone of Henrietta Sue, wife of James Aaron and
mother of Peter Aaron Jameson. He did the same with James
Aaron, husband of Henrietta Sue and father of Peter Aaron
Jameson. He approached Smiley's and she moved in closer.
She could feel her emotions reeling. There lay her father's
headstone. Peter Aaron Jameson, PVT, US Army, Born
1925, Died 1945, son of James Peter and Henrietta Sue
Jameson, and friend of Oliver Langdon. She looked up at the
old man. Tears streamed down his face. He turned his head
quickly.

"Mr. Langdon, you were obviously so much more than just a
friend to my father."

"Loved the boy and proud of him," he said with a broken
voice.

She took his arm. He put his hand over hers. They stood
together, admiring a young man whose life, different than
most, was one lived well and accomplished.

Their hold was broken as they moved away and returned to
the house. He picked up the framed photographs and they

walked back to the motel with no words spoken between them.

She had completed her journey here. She gave Mr. Langdon a note she had written earlier. It expressed her appreciation and included her contact information. She now thought it was so little compared to what he had given her.

He didn't look up, but said, "Good luck, girl," as he deposited the pictures at the door. And with that he walked away. She picked up the photos, entered the motel room, and put the framed pictures on the inexpensive dresser. She sat at the foot of the bed, staring into them. Just a couple of months ago she was Nicki Boyer and little did she know that her life story would include the images of the people before her. She was now Nicole Collette Jameson Boyer.

CHAPTER FIFTEEN

NICOLE COLLETTE BOYER

She arrived at her parents' home after dark. Leaving the pictures in the car, she greeted her parents and told them it was late, and she would let them know about the trip in the morning. The next day, she told them all about the discoveries and showed them the photographs she had been given. She was concerned that they might be uncomfortable with the details, but they instead remarked about the resemblance and how it gave them comfort to see a photograph of the man whose daughter became theirs. The three had a good cry before she left to return home to Houston.

She could hardly wait to call Brent, and as soon as she unpacked, she dispensed with her regular routine and called before she put everything away.

"Brent, it's Nicole. I'm back in Houston. I just can't wait to tell you all about Smiley," she said enthusiastically.

"Smiley?" he asked.

"That was the nickname of my father. Oh, Brent, he was such a fine man. There is more but I really need to tell you in person. And Brent, I have pictures!"

"I can hardly wait to hear all about it and see the photos," Brent exclaimed.

"Then come for a visit. I really hope you can get away for a while."

"I'll see what I can do. I am so anxious to see you, Nicole."

Within days, Brent was at her door. They embraced briefly, but even so, she could feel her body responding to his touch. She was genuinely glad to see him and have him in her life.

She showed him the photos and explained again how they became hers. She told him of Oliver Langdon and how she had realized what an integral part he had been in her father's life. She revealed a side of herself that she had not shown before. For the next few days, they were inseparable. Dinner and drinks were often followed by a romantic interlude at her place and when he had to return to Dallas, it was painful for both of them.

She had a few days of leave left and Brent had been gone for three days, leaving her to study the enormity of her discoveries. She still was not ready to return to work. She had something on her mind and picked up the phone.

"Brent, call me crazy, but I want to do something and I want you to do it with me."

"Sure. What's up?"

"I want to take you to the cemetery to see my father's headstone. I can't ask my parents to do it, but you are now part of my life and my life was due to the person in that cemetery. Will you make a trip with me?"

"You want to go back so soon?" he asked.

"Yes, I need to do this, maybe this one last time. Will you go?"

"Of course, let me make the arrangements."

Three days later, Nicole and Brent were approaching the little town of Larkspur.

"Walk with me," she said. He took her hand. Together, they followed the narrow road to the house, and she directed him to the path of the cemetery. As they got closer, she squinted. Something was unusual. When they came closer to the small cemetery, she could hardly believe her eyes. The cemetery had been cleared. Wildflowers had been planted all around the outside of the fence. Two small American flags were put on either side of her father's headstone.

Nicole clasped Brent's hand and glanced down. There, in the corner, stood a small metal sign, the ones used as temporary markers until a permanent headstone is erected. The sign read, "Oliver Langdon, 1978." She was filled with sadness. She knew he was elderly, but apparently, the memories she had brought back had taken a toll on him. She knew it was he who had taken care of the small plot, perhaps in preparation of his own arrival. She smiled and was filled with love. She bent over, and cleared the dirt that was smeared on the marker.

Brushing her hands together, she looked into Brent's eyes as he wrapped his arm around her waist. "We can go home now," she said as she maintained her pose. "I have an idea," he spoke. "Let's get married, right away, right here in Larkspur, and I know just the place for the honeymoon - PARIS."

She smiled. There was yet another chapter in the life of Nicole Collette Boyer. ♥♥

Made in the USA
San Bernardino, CA
07 May 2019